S0-BUA-600

# "Make up your mind. If you don't want to buy it, somebody else will.

It's a gamble, McDormand, but it's your choice. Do you want the stuff or not?"

Melissa's heart began to beat uncomfortably fast. She noticed that Greg's eyes looked yellow. Yellow-tinged eyes indicated heavy steroid use, and she had heard of 'roid rages, the sudden outbursts of violent temper that steroids could produce. "Okay. Okay," she said. "Don't get excited."

Greg's angry face relented. "Sorry. Sometimes I get a little hostile. Nothing personal. It's just the 'roids. Ever happen to you?"

Melissa laughed. "No. I've always had a little problem with my temper, but so far, no 'roid rages. Though you may see me have one on Saturday if I don't win. So I'll buy."

"All right!" Greg said. "You want some right now?"

Melissa nodded. The sooner she started medicating, the better. Saturday wasn't that far away.

Don't miss these books
in the exciting FRESHMAN DORM series

*Freshman Dorm*
*Freshman Lies*
*Freshman Guys*
*Freshman Nights*
*Freshman Dreams*
*Freshman Games*
*Freshman Loves*
*Freshman Secrets*
*Freshman Schemes*
*Freshman Changes*
*Freshman Fling*
*Freshman Rivals*
*Freshman Heartbreak*
*Freshman Flames*
*Freshman Choices*
*Freshman Feud*
*Freshman Follies*
*Freshman Wedding*
*Freshman Promises*
*Freshman Summer*
*Freshman Affair*
*Freshman Truths*
*Freshman Scandal*
*Freshman Christmas*
*Freshman Roommate*

And, coming soon . . .

*Freshman Heat*

**ATTENTION: ORGANIZATIONS AND CORPORATIONS**

Most HarperPaperbacks are available at special quantity dis-
counts for bulk purchases for sales promotions, premiums, or
fund-raising. For information, please call or write:
**Special Markets Department, HarperCollins Publishers,**
**10 East 53rd Street, New York, N.Y. 10022.**
**Telephone: (212) 207-7528. Fax: (212) 207-7222.**

# FRESHMAN OBSESSION

## LINDA A. COONEY

### HarperPaperbacks
*A Division of HarperCollinsPublishers*

If you purchased this book without a cover, you should be aware that this book is stolen property. It was reported as "unsold and destroyed" to the publisher and neither the author nor the publisher has received any payment for this "stripped book."

This is a work of fiction. The characters, incidents, and dialogues are products of the author's imagination and are not to be construed as real. Any resemblance to actual events or persons, living or dead, is entirely coincidental.

HarperPaperbacks   *A Division of* HarperCollins*Publishers*
10 East 53rd Street, New York, N.Y. 10022

Copyright © 1993 by Linda Alper and Kevin Cooney
All rights reserved. No part of this book may be used or reproduced in any manner whatsoever without written permission of the publisher, except in the case of brief quotations embodied in critical articles and reviews. For information address HarperCollins*Publishers,*
10 East 53rd Street, New York, N.Y. 10022.

Cover illustration by Tony Greco

First printing: February 1993

Printed in the United States of America

HarperPaperbacks and colophon are trademarks of HarperCollins*Publishers*

❖ 10 9 8 7 6 5 4 3 2 1

# One
.................

"**M**elissa McDormand, get out of that bed *now*!" Caitlin Bruneau ordered.

Melissa lifted her head an inch off her pillow and half opened one eye. "Give me one good reason why I should," she grumbled.

"Well, for starters, the Board of Health is going to evict you if you don't clean up this place." Caitlin looked around Melissa's dorm room and cringed in disgust. Magazines and half-empty chip bags littered the floor. One of Melissa's premed anatomy models had tipped over and looked like it was diving into an empty doughnut box. Instead of her usual chemistry and biology books, a TV guide lay open on her desk.

"I'm a wreck," Melissa muttered. "I'm tired. I feel awful. I have no friends anymore, and the whole world sucks. Other than that, everything's fine." She sat up. "You still haven't given me a good reason why I should get out of bed."

"I'll give you a good reason," Caitlin barked. "There are some big track meets coming up later this spring. Big meets. The winners of the last meet will go on to the Olympic trials. You're one of the best runners we have. The team needs you."

"You don't need me," Melissa wept, burrowing down deeper under the blanket. "No one needs me."

"Stop acting so pathetic," Caitlin ordered.

"What do you care?" Melissa pulled the sheet over her head. Melissa had been in bed for four days straight. Her short red hair was sticking to her forehead. Her face was so pale that her freckles had practically disappeared. Her usually strong runner's legs felt like they were made of bread dough.

"Melissa," Caitlin said with a sigh. "The coach needs you. You've got to snap out of it!"

"Brooks Baldwin didn't need me," Melissa argued. "If he'd needed me, or wanted me, or even just decided to be decent to me, he wouldn't have left me standing at the altar in a stupid wedding dress. He wouldn't have set me up just to dump me. Just when I really believed that he loved me, Brooks changed his mind and walked out of my life."

Caitlin's hard expression softened at the reminder of Melissa's story. "I know all that."

"Of course you know it!" Melissa screamed. "Probably everyone in the world knows it! I'll never show my face at this university again." She buried her face in her hands and indulged in a fresh stream of moans and tears. With each sob she remembered Brooks's handsome, double-crossing face. With each soggy tear she saw the stunned, embarrassed expressions of her dorm friends, and her roommate, Lauren Turnbell-Smythe. She hated their pity and their stares. She just wanted to be left alone!

Melissa felt Caitlin's hand shake her shoulder. She suddenly realized how odd it was for Caitlin to be comforting her. She and Caitlin had been bitter rivals in the 800-meter. Since then, Caitlin had been dropped from the 800 and put on shorter distances. Caitlin was also the team captain now, and had taken on a coach-like pride in the entire team.

"Look," Caitlin said awkwardly. "I know we haven't been very close."

Melissa snorted.

"In fact, we were pretty hard on each other when we ran the same event. But I don't care about that anymore. I want our whole team to do well." She shook her head. "Besides, you can't spend the rest of your life hiding in this room, crying, and eating Twinkies."

"I haven't been eating Twinkies." Even as she said it, Melissa noticed a Mrs. Wise's Giant Cookie wrapper clinging to the edge of her blanket. Okay, so she had been filling her emptiness by chomping chocolate chips. For a while, her roommate Lauren had joined her in her eating fest. But then Lauren had rejected Melissa, too. At least Twinkies and Snickers bars didn't give you dirty looks or give you stupid advice about "just getting over it."

Caitlin sat on Melissa's bed. She focused her eyes sternly on Melissa. "Listen. We're both runners. Good runners. And I think that in some ways, we understand each other better than anyone else does."

Melissa shrugged.

"Take it from me," Caitlin continued. "The best way, the only way, to stop feeling like a loser is to get out there and start winning again."

Melissa forced a laugh. "What a great idea, Caitlin. There's only one little problem. How am I supposed to win now when my mind is like mud, my heart is empty, and my legs feel like Jell-O?"

Caitlin didn't answer.

Melissa threw back her covers to reveal her pale body, dressed in old track shorts and a T-shirt. She hadn't really gotten fat. Not yet. But her overdeveloped muscles had drooped and softened. She looked saggy and almost gray.

Caitlin stared. Then she let out a big sigh and got up from the bed. She took three steps toward the door, then stopped. For a long moment she stood there, with her back to Melissa, as if she were a sign post. When she turned back she was wearing the "win or die" look that Melissa remembered from so many meets. "There is something you can do," she said.

"What?" Melissa whispered, intrigued by the purpose in Caitlin's face.

"If you really want to be a winner," Caitlin said in a husky voice, "then you do whatever you have to do. You take shortcuts. You get help. You do it. It just depends on how much you want to win."

Melissa swallowed. *Winning*. Just the word made some part of her come back to life. If she could just *win* again, then maybe the rest of her painful past would disappear.

"Well?" Caitlin prompted. "Is that what you want? Do you still want to win?"

Melissa took a deep breath. "Of course I want to win. I want to win more than anything else in the world."

"That's all I needed to hear." Caitlin smiled. "I know how to help you. Promise me you won't tell anyone, and then just do what I say. . . ."

\*    \*    \*

One day later that spring, Melissa was jogging easily down the brightly lit hallways of the sprawling University of Springfield athletic complex. She felt confident, strong, and light. She glanced down at her tanned legs. As she ran, each well defined muscle contracted, then bulged. She pumped her arms, which were also toned and strong. She felt as if she had enough energy to run laps around the moon.

"Thank you, Caitlin, my pal," Melissa giggled to herself. She grinned as she hurdled a wooden bench. She kept running, feeling as if she could travel the hall in one leap.

Caitlin and Melissa were about to run for a place in the pre-Olympic trial. If they won that day, then they would race again the next Saturday for the biggest prize—a chance to try the raceway to Olympic fame, fortune, and running-shoe endorsements—as the guys on the team liked to say.

Melissa jogged past two pole-vaulters stretching in the hallway outside the men's locker room. She opened a creaky metal door, then jogged down two sets of narrow stairs. The air turned colder. The concrete became more faded and cracked. When she opened a door again, she was in the gym basement.

"Over here!" Caitlin hissed. She was hiding behind a maze of heating ducts.

"Hi." Melissa smiled.

"What took you so long!" Caitlin answered in a frantic voice. She was dressed in her jersey and shorts, her number already pinned on her back. She was slim, but looked stunningly strong. Each muscle in her legs stood out as if it had been carved.

"What's up?" Melissa asked.

"We have to hurry," Caitlin blurted. "They're already starting the hundred-yard dash up in the stadium."

"Okay, so why did you so urgently want to see me?"

Caitlin jerked her head, indicating that she wanted Melissa to follow her. "Don't talk here," she said. "Too many people around the gym. There must be two hundred athletes from all over the state here today. We can't be too careful."

Wordlessly, Melissa followed Caitlin down the hall. They passed equipment-storage areas, the boiler room, and some old workout spaces that hadn't been used for years. "Why all the cloak-and-dagger?" Melissa protested.

"Shh!" Caitlin looked quickly around to be sure no one was watching, then pushed open an old wooden door.

Melissa kept up with Caitlin as she flew down one more set of stairs. This last set led to a tiny space that was underneath one corner of the large basement. It was a dark, deserted concrete cell that had once housed cleaning equipment for the swimming pool. It was closed up now and off limits but, in reality, it had become a kind of secret clubhouse.

Caitlin pulled Melissa into the room, then unzipped her gym bag. "Close the door."

Melissa pulled the door closed, and leaned against it. She noticed that someone had drawn the words 'Roid Dungeon in the dusty floor. She snickered. That was what they all called it—'roid dungeon, 'roid room, 'roid heaven. It was where athletes met to sell, discuss, and take the illegal drugs that made them stronger—anabolic steroids.

In the last month, Melissa had put on five pounds of pure muscle. She'd taken four seconds off her race time. Steroids were wonder drugs that had given her recent workouts that extra edge. They were the magic potion that had helped her bulk up, work hard, and get tough, so that she had quickly gotten back into fabulous shape.

Caitlin pulled out a vial and two disposable syringes. "Pull down the top of your shorts," she ordered. She quickly removed the paper cover from the needles, then stuck the needle into the top of the vial. She tipped the vial over and began pulling the liquid drug into the syringe.

Melissa was beginning to feel uneasy. Caitlin was

the first to admit she was no expert with this stuff. And they'd never injected right before a race. For weeks, she and Caitlin had been medicating every other day and only in the morning.

"But . . ." Melissa objected.

"Just do it!" Caitlin barked. She checked her watch. Sweat had popped out all over her face, and a vein throbbed across her forehead. "We've got to be back on the field in five minutes. I don't have time to argue or explain. You're just going to have to trust me. Have I let you down yet?"

Melissa shook her head. She tugged down the waistband of her U of S warmup pants and gym shorts. Caitlin ripped open an individually packaged antiseptic pad and cleaned the skin on the back of Melissa's hip. Melissa waited for the needle's sting and reminded herself that, so far, everything Caitlin had promised had come true. Melissa was getting stronger and faster every day.

*ZAP!*

"Ouch." Melissa flinched as the sharp needle poked through her skin.

"Now you do me," Caitlin said. She thrust a syringe into Melissa's hands. Melissa pursed her lips. She hesitated a little, then plunged the needle into Caitlin's muscular hip. Her stomach clenched when she pulled the needle out. Get used to it, she told herself sternly. Someday, when you're a doctor, you're going to be doing a lot of this.

Caitlin rearranged her waistband almost before Melissa had time to put the cap back on the needle. "Hurry!" she urged. She and Melissa threw the used works into Caitlin's gym bag for disposal later. "Let's get out of here," Caitlin said breathlessly, scooping up the bag and running toward the door.

Minutes later, Melissa and Caitlin were back up on the ground floor of the athletic complex and barreling out the gym's front door. They could hear the rumble of the crowd and the amplified voice of the announcer. Melissa took a few deep breaths of the crisp mountain air and waited for the familiar "pump" the steroids usually produced. But she wasn't feeling it. Maybe this new steroid had a delayed reaction.

Caitlin raced on ahead and Melissa jogged behind her, across the parking lot and toward the athletes' entrance to the stadium. They wove around double-parked cars and big silver charter buses that had transported all the top track-and-field athletes from all over the state. They hurried to the athletes' entrance and caught sight of the green field, surrounded by the oval cinder track.

Caitlin gave Melissa a relieved smile. "Well. Here we are."

"Here we are." Melissa turned to glance up into the

bleachers, taking in the faces, the hand-painted signs and banners, the blue sky, and the bright sun overhead. The place was packed. Field events were already taking place on the grass. Melissa suddenly remembered lying limply in her bed such a short time ago, feeling like she would never face the world again.

She reached for Caitlin's hand. "Thanks," she said. "If it weren't for you, I wouldn't be here."

Caitlin reached for Melissa and they threw their arms around each other. "Run a good race," Caitlin whispered. "Just do it. Fly. Don't think. Just run."

"You, too," Melissa answered. They held each other, then broke apart, giving each other the thumbs-up sign.

Caitlin peeled away to join the sprinters, and Melissa headed for the area of the sidelines where the 800-meter runners were bending and stretching. Two of her opponents were from her own team, but most were from other schools. The girls barely looked at one another. They all knew the odds. The top three runners from each race would go on to the pre-Olympic trials. The rest of them would sit in the bleachers and watch.

Melissa peeled off her warm up pants. She bent over, stretching out the muscles in her back. Still no pump, but that was okay. She was pumped enough with nervous anticipation. She bent her left leg and leaned heavily on the right one. She remembered that she'd injured her right Achilles tendon that winter and checked to make sure there was no weakness now. She circled her foot, then lunged and touched her forehead to her knee. She felt great. No pain. No doubt. Just strength and speed and the desire to win so bad that it hurt.

"YAY, MELISSA!"

"GO, MEL!"

"MELIIIIIIIISSSAAAA!"

Melissa tipped her head up. The chorus of voices had come from the bleachers nearby. When she saw the row of familiar faces she wasn't sure whether to glare or grin. KC Angeletti sat next to her boyfriend, radio DJ Cody Wainwright. Winnie Gottlieb, Melissa's old roommate, was bouncing between KC and Winnie's new husband, Josh Gaffey. Even from down on the field, Melissa could make out Winnie's leopard-print tank top and a hat that had foam deer antlers.

Lauren Turnbull-Smythe, Melissa's current roommate, sat in the row in front of Josh, wearing a jumpsuit and marking notes in a little pad.

"YAY, MELISSA!" they all cried again, waving their U of S pennants at her.

Melissa stretched again so she wouldn't have to wave back. She was glad to know that they were there. But it hurt, too. All those people had been her friends once. Most of them had been there to see her get dumped at the altar. But after the fiasco of her wedding day, those friendships had pretty much come to an end. Every time they tried to get close, Melissa had seen the pity in their eyes. She didn't want pity, she told herself. No, she wanted an Olympic medal. If she made it to the Olympics, nobody would ever feel sorry for her again.

Melissa straightened up, feeling strong and single-minded again. She took one last glance at her friends, and then her heart plummeted down into her shoes. A couple of rows behind Lauren, Melissa spotted a boy with blond hair and an uncomplicated, hand-some face. He wore a rugby shirt and baseball cap, and had his chin leaning on his hand.

Brooks.

Humiliation rushed through Melissa's body. She squeezed her eyes shut. Terry Meecham, her track coach, was always telling her that the mind was the most powerful muscle of them all. *Utilize. Visualize. Concentrate.* Melissa used her mind to banish the thought of Brooks and to imagine an Olympic gold medal on her chest.

Slowly she exhaled. The hurt was gone for now. Melissa opened her eyes and blinked. When she focused on the field, she saw that the women's 400 was in progress. She saw Caitlin come sprinting down the last lap, racing across the finish line in second place! There was a roar from the crowd.

"YES, CAIT!" Melissa's heart swelled and she lifted

her fist, pumping it high in the air for her friend. "That's it. Winnnerrrr. That's the way!"

"FIRST CALL FOR THE WOMEN'S 800," blared the loudspeaker. Melissa's heart began to pound. Showtime, she thought, hurrying toward the starting line with the other middle-distance runners. She took her place and shook out her arms and legs. Then she began another round of deep breathing.

"LAST CALL FOR THE WOMEN'S 800."

Coach Terry waved to her from the fence. "This is your race, McDormand," he called. "Think it. Run it. Win it!"

Melissa nodded, feeling a rush of confidence. She'd never felt so eager. So ready.

"RUNNERS, TAKE YOUR MARKS!"

Melissa positioned her feet, placing her left foot ahead of her right.

CRAAAAAACK!

Melissa felt the sound of the starting gun explode inside her soul. Her legs sprang into action as she flew down the first straightway, staying with the pack. Her muscles begged to pull out ahead and lead the race, but her brain told her to bide her time. There were two runners she'd never seen before, a blonde from Weslin and a brunette from Western U. The pack of eight women thundered around the first curve, and just as Melissa had anticipated, the two wild cards pulled out ahead as the group pounded down the second straightway.

Melissa waited and waited. Just when she sensed that the front-runners were getting tired, she used her kick, pushing, driving, pounding the track until she was running a solid third. She veered into the next lane and pushed until she was running at the blonde's elbow and could hear her breathing. Then she really poured on the speed, pumping and churning. She sailed past the blonde and eyed the brunette in the lead, gauging her speed and preparing to make her move. She lowered her head slightly, then moved into overdrive, exhorting every muscle to action. She could see the arms and legs of the front runner as if they were moving in slow motion. They were both going for the gold.

Melissa began to be aware of her feet, pounding harder and harder against the ground. The white tape gleamed whiter. Melissa gave it everything she had. She lowered her head and threw herself forward, breaking the tape a fraction of a second ahead of the front runner.

"YAAAAAAAAAAY!"

"MELL . . . ISSSSSS . . . AAAAAAAAA!"

The air in the stadium seemed to vibrate as the crowd went wild. Melissa raised her hands over her head and leaped into the air. First! She'd finished first! Tears welled in her eyes and spilled down her cheeks as she continued around the oval, waving her hand in the air.

"YAY, MELISSA!" Winnie Gottlieb's shrill scream

pierced the air. Through her tears, Melissa saw her old friends frantically waving their banners. Even Brooks was standing up, waving and yelling. Melissa flashed a smile in their direction, then jogged over toward Terry Meecham.

Caitlin stood just outside the huddle. She grabbed Melissa's upper arm before Melissa could reach Terry. But she didn't hug or congratulate her. If fact, she looked like they'd both just come in last.

Melissa winced as Caitlin's fingers dug painfully into the muscle of her arm. "What's wrong?"

"Drug test," Caitlin said in a deadly voice.

Melissa felt like Caitlin had just pounded her on the head with a sledgehammer. She felt a wave of dizziness and her knees buckled. She would have fallen if Caitlin hadn't tightened her grip on her arm, holding her upright.

"Problem, McDormand?" she heard Terry ask. "We need to do a urine test. It's routine. You and Bruneau can spare some of your precious liquids, can't you?"

Melissa shook herself. "No problem," she managed to say through lips that were suddenly paper dry. "I just . . ."

Terry grinned. "You did great, McDormand. You too, Captain Bruneau. I'll give the strokes and a few suggestions later on. Right now, race over into the gym for a stupid drug test. I don't like this any more than you do, but if the Athletic Commission wants to spot check, we have to cooperate."

# Two
..............

"All right, Melissa!" Faith Crowley screamed happily as the meet results were being announced over the campus radio station.

Faith clicked off the radio, pushed her long blonde braid off her shoulder, and wished for a brief moment that she had gone to the meet. It would have been nice to be there to yell for Melissa in person. But Faith had too many things to do—which was why she was sitting cross-legged on Becker Cain's bed in his single study-dorm room with a play script in her lap. Becker had given her a key to his room, and his study-dorm offered fewer distractions than her own room at Coleridge Hall, the creative-arts dorm.

Faith looked around Becker's immaculate room, thinking how different it was from the space she shared with her fellow Theater-Arts major, Liza Ruff. Their room generally looked like somebody had dropped a hand grenade in the middle of it—or at least Liza's half. Becker's room was monastic by comparison. White walls. A built-in desk. One lamp. Except for the large poster with a question mark on it, there was no decoration at all. Philosophy major Becker had very few possessions. He said he didn't need them. His world was the world of the mind—and the body.

*And what a body,* she thought. Becker had been Faith's platonic roommate during a week-long co-ed by bed experiment. They'd talked a lot and studied into the late hours. By the end of the experiment, their feelings for each other were far from platonic.

Faith checked her watch, which she always wore now, since Becker didn't believe in clocks. She wished that he'd get back from his honors philosophy seminar.

"So, Becker, where are you?" she asked out loud. Sure, she wanted to concentrate and study, but she was also eager to show Becker the formal letter of acceptance she had received to the University of

Springfield's Professional Theatre Program. Becker had helped her get into the program, which would allow her to spend sophomore year with a select group of students and well-known guest faculty.

Finally Faith heard the rattle of the doorknob. Her pulse quickened. She jumped up and tugged down her cotton sweater.

The door swung open. Faith watched Becker stop in the doorway with the aura of complete self-possession that made him seem older than a sophomore. Just looking at Becker made her feel giddy. He was tall and lanky, but with broad shoulders and strong, elegant hands. His jeans were crisp and unfaded. His white shirt was starched and his hair was long. Little round wire-rimmed glasses gave his aristocratic face a touch of eccentricity. As usual, he carried about fifteen pounds of books.

"You're back," she said.

"If I'd known you were going to be here, I'd have come back sooner." He shut the door and moved immediately toward her as if she were a magnet and he was a hunk of metal. When he sat down on the bed, Faith leaned against his arm. He nudged her, and then she nudged him. She laughed, then stopped laughing when he ran his hand down her bare arms.

"Are you cold?" he asked his deep, calm voice.

Faith shook her head. "Not now." She stretched out on the bed and felt his warm hands as he began to rub the back of her neck, then massage her whole back. Starting to giggle, she snapped her fingers. "Don't forget the soles of my feet, sir, while you're at it," she teased in a British accent.

Without hesitation, Becker scrambled around, pushed his stack of books away, and began rubbing the bottoms of her feet. He massaged her heels, her toes. "You know, some people think that the soles of your feet are the link to your whole body," he said.

Faith laughed. She was beginning to feel as if she had no feet. She was floating, footless, on a warm cloud. "Or the feet are the window on the sole. S.O.L.E., I mean." She laughed at her own joke. "I know puns are the lowest form of humor, Beck, but I couldn't resist."

He climbed up next to her and kissed her neck. "I know the feeling," he breathed.

Becker looked at her with his you-are-the-only-person-in-my-world eyes, then kissed her slowly. Faith was so overwhelmed that she started to laugh in the middle of his kiss. She could feel his arms encircle her, his slim body slide onto the bed. It was either giggle or completely give in and go further than she was ready to go . . . yet. She tried to catch her breath.

As usual, Becker immediately picked up on her signal. He sat up and smiled, too. "Did you have an interesting afternoon?" he asked.

Faith sat up, too, and smoothed her long hair. Her french braid was now a disaster with its wisps of stray hairs. She still felt giddy and slightly off-balance. "Yes," she said, trying hard to clear the fog that had descended around her brain. "Did you?"

"I don't want to talk about me," he said. "What happened for you today?"

"Melissa McDormand won the 800."

"That's not you," he pointed out. "That's Melissa."

Faith shrugged. Becker didn't have the slightest idea of why Melissa's win was so important. He never paid attention to sports. "That means she'll be in the Olympic trials next Saturday."

"So?"

"So, Beck. She's my friend. At least she used to be my friend."

He gave her a quizzical smile. "And does her winning make you happy?"

"Yeah, I think it does."

He shrugged and smiled. "Then it makes me happy, too." He waved a finger. "Yay, Melissa." And with that, he pushed Faith back down on the bed and stared down into her face. "Now enough about Melissa McDormand," he growled. "Tell me more about the only person who matters here, the only person in my life. Tell me about you."

Faith squirmed away from him, laughing as he

grabbed for her elbow, and reached for the letter that was tucked inside her copy of Shakespeare's *The Taming of the Shrew*. "I got this today," she sang coyly. She dropped the letter over Becker's head.

Becker caught the paper before it landed on his hair. "Don't tell me," he smiled. "It's your friends again. This is from your old friend, Winnie. She's running away from Josh to join the circus. She wants you to go with her."

Faith shook her head. "Not this time."

Becker pretended to think harder. "Maybe it's from KC, and she's offering you the investment opportunity of a lifetime. Fifty shares of the Brooklyn Bridge. Or it's from Lauren. She's off to war-torn Upper Slabovia to be a battlefield correspondent, and she wants to know if she can borrow your canteen. Or maybe it's from Brooks. He's decided that . . ."

"Okay, Becker." Faith sighed. She was starting to find him less funny now. He'd insisted that her old friends weren't good for her, that they just wanted to use her. He'd turned out to be right. Horrifyingly right. Winnie, Lauren, and Brooks had all pulled outrageous and thoughtless stunts, imposing on Faith's friendship and not giving a single thought to Faith's own needs. Even so, she hadn't liked cutting off her friends, though it had been necessary.

"You don't miss them, do you?" Becker asked.

Faith shook her head. It was Becker who had finally forced her to realize how chaotic and unproductive her life had become—largely due to her so-called friends. Finally, she'd really let them have it, and she'd told them to keep their distance. She just had to have some time for herself these days. And for Becker.

Becker rolled onto his side and propped himself up on one elbow. He opened her letter and began to read.

Faith perched on her knees to look over his shoulder. "It's my formal acceptance letter to the Professional Theatre Program," she blurted. "I'm definitely in."

"Oh," he said brightly. "But you already knew that, didn't you?" He looked back at her and kissed her arm.

Faith nodded and leaned over him. "But having it in writing just makes it feel real. Thanks for helping me get in."

"I only wish I could help you get everything you ever wanted, everything you ever will want," he murmured, kissing her again.

Faith blushed and gave in to his kisses for a while. She wasn't sure what was more intoxicating, his physical attentions, or the way he'd helped her impress the theater-arts faculty and get into the program as a mere freshman. Her interview had required her to come up with an original directing concept for *The Taming of the Shrew*. But between her friends' neediness and her own mental block, she hadn't come up with a single idea. At the last minute, it had been Becker who'd suggested a wild west *Taming of the Shrew*.

Faith touched her nose to Becker's. "How can I ever thank you?" she murmured. She stared into his eyes.

"I don't expect to be thanked," he said quietly. Then he rolled over to face her. He touched her face with both hands. The sudden seriousness in his eyes frightened Faith just a little.

She held her breath.

Becker closed his eyes. "I helped you for only one reason, Faith," he said in a low voice. "I did it because I love you. Maybe I've always loved you. I love you more than I love anyone else or anything, and I always will. I will do anything—anything—to help you get what you want."

Faith's heart stopped for a moment. There was no way she could laugh this time, and yet that was just what she wanted to do. Why and how had Becker suddenly gotten so serious? How could he love her more than anyone he'd ever known, or would know. "We haven't known each other very long," she said.

"That doesn't matter," he said, pulling her closer. "Not to me. I know exactly how I feel. And I know exactly what I want. And I know what you want. And I'll always figure out how to get it."

Faith didn't move. She barely breathed. She just

looked into Becker's intelligent eyes, trying to ignore the sudden twinge of fear she felt deep inside.

Melissa's fear flooded her whole body as she sat in the waiting area of the gym testing center. Her fingers were clasped tightly in her lap to keep her hands from shaking. Her brain was in overdrive. *I'll be suspended from the athletic program,* she kept thinking. *I'll lose my scholarship. By tonight, I'll be looking for a job as a waitress or a maid.*

Caitlin sat next to Melissa. Her body was slick with nervous sweat and the backs of her strong legs looked like they were glued to the seat of her molded plastic orange chair.

Melissa sighed and glanced at Caitlin.

Caitlin swallowed visibly, then looked down at her lap.

A couple of hurdlers, all the discus and javelin throwers, a few long jumpers, and most of the runners had been rounded up and herded to the gym. They'd all given urine samples and now they were waiting for the results. Most people wandered and joked. Some, like Melissa and Caitlin, sat pretending to rest or meditate. Those were the jocks that Melissa recognized from the 'roid dungeon. She could tell by their faces that they were as terrified as she.

"We've been here for an hour," Melissa finally said, breaking the silence between her and Caitlin.

"I know," Caitlin said. "Try to stay cool. Think about something else."

Melissa stared out the one big window, but the only thing she could think about was Brooks and her ex-friends. If she were caught, they'd think she was helpless. She can't hold onto her fiancé, and now she can't even keep her track title. Melissa cringed and stared out the window again.

She could see dark clouds gathering around the peaks of the mountains. It looked like it might rain. *That would be an appropriate ending to my day,* she thought miserably. *An appropriate ending to my whole life.*

Melissa looked at Caitlin. Suddenly it all seemed insane. What were they doing sitting like lambs waiting for the slaughter? Melissa had to get out of here. She wasn't going to wait for the ax to fall. She had to run, to hide. Her stomach lurched and she stood up.

But as she took a step, the door to the gym's inner office opened. Every muscle in the room tensed. Caitlin seemed to stop breathing. An official from the athletic association walked slowly into the gym. He was tall, with gray hair and shaggy eyebrows. He looked down at his clipboard and his brow furrowed.

No one said a word. But every eye was riveted to

his clipboard. The official cleared his throat. Melissa's legs began to shake.

"As I'm sure you are all aware," the doctor began, "anabolic steroids are extremely dangerous drugs. They produce changes in the body and the mind which can sometimes be irreversible, and do not, repeat, *do not* justify the short-term gains of increased strength. In addition, using drugs is unfair, unsportsmanslike, and illegal."

His eyes swept the room and seemed to rest on Melissa and Caitlin. Melissa's heart began to race and she felt the color drain from her face.

The official looked down at his clipboard again. "But I am happy to report that every athlete at this meet tested negative."

NEGATIVE!

The official smiled. "We have a clean competition here and I want to keep it that way. Congratulations on your achievements this afternoon. Continue to train safely and wisely. You may go."

Melissa felt the tension flow out of her like air escaping from a balloon. But she was completely bewildered. How in the world could her test have come out negative? Was this a dream? A joke? A nightmare?

Caitlin let out her breath in a long sigh, as did several other people in the room. "Let's go," she said to Melissa.

Melissa tried to stand, but her legs felt wobbly. "What happened?" she whispered. "How . . . What . . . I don't get . . ."

"I'll tell you outside," Caitlin whispered in return. "Pull yourself together."

Melissa managed to stand on her shaking legs and started to walk out. She felt the strength returning to her muscles as she and Caitlin traveled the long corridor that led to the front door. Finally, they stepped out into the open air.

When the last athlete had passed safely out of earshot, Caitlin turned to Melissa and grinned. "It worked," she said in a voice of deep satisfaction.

"What worked?" Melissa demanded. "What's going on?"

Caitlin grabbed Melissa's arm. "What we injected before the race wasn't a steroid," she told Melissa. "It was a drug to mask the steroids so that they couldn't be detected in a urine test."

"Masking drugs! Is there such a thing?"

Caitlin nodded. "I didn't have time to explain it, or argue with you earlier. There were rumors that there might be a drug test after this meet. Somebody drove out to Oregon last night, made the buy, and got back with the stuff early this morning. But nobody knew for sure whether or not it would work." She shrugged. "There's a lot of guesswork in this."

"Why didn't you tell me?" Melissa exploded.

"Look," Caitlin said. "I didn't know anything for sure and I didn't want to blow your concentration before the race."

Melissa took some deep breaths and began to shake out her arms. Her palms were still damp with anxiety and she wiped them on the seat of her warmup pants. Masking drugs. Surprise drug tests. Guesswork. She'd always known she was taking a risk. But she'd never really realized until today how real the dangers were. "I don't know about this anymore," she said, swallowing hard, trying to force some moisture into her mouth. "I don't know if I can go through something like this again. It's not worth it."

"Not worth it!" Caitlin cried angrily. "Not *worth* it? Get your priorities straight, McDormand."

Caitlin took a step forward and Melissa saw her hands ball into angry fists.

Melissa took a step back, but she'd balled her own hands into fists, too. It wasn't the first time she'd noticed that Caitlin seemed ready to fly off the handle at the tiniest provocation. That was definitely a result of the steroids. Her own anger was always boiling just below the surface.

Melissa and Caitlin stood in a face-off. But instead of an explosion of anger, there was a sudden clap of thunder. A moment later a hard, fresh, cool rain began to fall and the tension broke.

Caitlin threw her head back, letting the rain splash down on her face. "Go ahead," she shouted at the sky. "Rain all you want. I'm a winner and I won't melt."

Melissa turned her face up to the sky, too. She felt the spring rain pour down, washing away the perspiration and the tension of the day. Suddenly, her heart lifted and soared. Caitlin was right, she decided. She'd survived a lot in her life. And she'd keep on surviving. She wouldn't just survive; she'd go all the way to the top.

A crack of lightning split the sky, briefly illuminating the mountain peaks in the distance and the roofs of the tallest campus buildings. In spite of the violent storm, Melissa felt more confident than she ever had in her whole life. She began to laugh, and she and Caitlin began to do a crazy rain dance.

What were the chances of being tested again? Probably zilch, Melissa decided. She hooted and looked up at the sky. Lightning never struck in the same place twice.

# Three

························

auren Turnbell-Smythe strolled around the back of Mill Pond. As she neared the dock, she looked out over the blue water. Students in canoes splashed each other with paddles. The sound of their happy laughter floated toward her.

Lauren pushed her wispy blonde hair back from her face and turned her large, violet eyes upward. The previous day's storm had blown every cloud out of the sky, and now it seemed like the entire campus was in a sunny mood. Even Melissa had seemed friendly and happy that morning when Lauren had congratulated her on her win.

Lauren sighed, thinking about Melissa. It would be nice if she and her roommate could finally bury the hatchet and make up. They had been at odds for a long time. Lauren realized they'd each been angry at the men in their lives and they'd taken it out on each other.

Lauren kept walking. She rubbed her cheek against the shoulder of her soft, brushed-cotton shirt. She was tired of being angry at men. Tired of being angry at everybody. And tired of having people angry at her.

Especially Faith.

"Hi, everybody!" Lauren called, spotting her friends, who were waiting for her near the boathouse.

As she hurried to join them, she thought back to the beginning of her freshman year. She'd been so shy and insecure, she could hardly bring herself to speak to Faith, KC, and Winnie, who had all been best friends in high school. But Faith had pulled Lauren into their circle and little by little, Lauren had quit feeling plain and plump, and had begun to develop some confidence in herself. Lately, though, she had begun to go too far in the opposite direction. She'd become so assertive that she'd taken advantage of Faith, humiliated herself, and pushed Faith away.

"Lauren, we're all here. We're just waiting for you!" Winnie called out.

Lauren saw that everyone was waiting. KC and Cody were listening to a tape—probably a recording of

Cody's radio show. Winnie and Josh sat on the dock, laughing and giggling. As Lauren got closer she could hear that they were trying to come up with a name for the baby Winnie was expecting. She also noticed that Faith wasn't there. The famous trio was without its third part. It was pretty ironic. Over the course of their freshman year, Faith had patched up dozens of squabbles between Winnie and KC and between Lauren and KC. Now Lauren, Winnie, and KC were on good terms, and it was Faith who had angrily opted out of their group.

Lauren sighed and sat down on the wooden plank with her friends. "Hi, all," she said. But she could tell that everyone was listening to Winnie.

". . . or we could name the baby after me," Winnie was joking. "Then when its diapers are dirty, we could call it 'Winnie the Pooh'." As usual, Winnie's nonstop, chatter dominated the conversation. Even pregnancy hadn't managed to subdue her. Still looking slim, she was decked out in full Winnie regalia—bright purple tights, a tiger-print bodysuit, green track shorts, and plastic earrings shaped like bunches of bananas.

Cody flipped his long dark ponytail off of his shoulder and adjusted one of the wide silver bracelets he always wore. He put his small tape player back into his leather bag. "What about a fine old southern name like Bubba or Junior?" he suggested in his slow Tennessee drawl.

"I wouldn't mind giving the baby a name like Moonbeam or Rainbow." Josh ran a hand through his shaggy brown hair and adjusted his own bracelet, which was made of woven leather and blue beads. "You know, do the sixties thing."

"NO!" KC screamed. She pulled at her own long dark hair and twisted the classic features of her beautiful face into a look of comic horror. "Don't do it. Please. Take it from me, Kahia Cayenne Angeletti, totally mainstream daughter of unreconstructed hippies."

Lauren laughed.

KC smoothed her plaid wool skirt and adjusted the lapels of her blazer. "He'll hate it, or she'll hate it, just like I did. Lauren! Think of a name before Winnie's poor baby gets stuck with Moonbeam."

Lauren smiled at the four friendly faces that appealed to her for a suggestion. "I'm not very good at coming up with names," she answered softly. She loved Winnie and Josh, but she couldn't help thinking that this baby may not be such a wonderful thing. Winnie was still awfully young, and she and Josh hadn't been married very long. A baby was a tie that would bind Winnie to Josh forever, making her even more dependent on him than she already was.

"Come on, Lauren," Josh pleaded. He reached over to poke her.

"Hey, how about literary names," Winnie said. "Lauren, you'd know about that."

"Charles Dickens Gaffey," Josh suggested.

KC laughed. "Jane Austin Gaffey."

"Balzac Gaffey," Cody said, and they all laughed.

Lauren couldn't join in the fun. After her off again, on again relationship with newspaper editor Dash Ramirez, Lauren didn't trust committed relationships. At least she had learned an important lesson about men. They weren't very dependable. Sure, she'd gone over the top as a militant feminist. But she was still a feminist—just maybe without the militant. Or maybe she was a militant friend now instead. Friends had to look out for each other—which was why Lauren had called this meeting of Faith's friends.

Lauren checked her watch. "We're almost all here. Has anyone seen Brooks?"

Right on cue, Brooks came ambling toward the group. He carried a backpack and had drafting pencils stuffed in the pockets of his hiking shorts.

"Hi," Brooks said uncertainly. His nose was sunburned and starting to peel. He darted a quick look at Lauren. "Sorry I'm late. My architecture class ran ten minutes over. I got here as soon as I could."

Lauren nodded. "Thanks."

"Hi, everybody," Brooks said good naturedly. He looked around, shook hands with Cody, then sat down next to KC. "So, what's this meeting about, Lauren?"

"Yeah," Winnie laughed. "Spill the beans already." She looked over at Brooks. "Lauren said she wasn't going to tell us anything until everybody was here."

Lauren looked at each member of the group for a moment. "This meeting is about Faith," she said simply.

Winnie and Brooks looked down at the dock.

Lauren cleared her throat. "We've spent a lot of our freshman year dragging Faith into our problems, leaning on her. And what's finally come of it? She's sick of all of us, and suddenly she spends all her time with Becker Cain."

Brooks picked up a leaf and crunched it in his hand.

Lauren plunged ahead. She'd already gone out on a limb to call this meeting. There was no wimping out now. "Anyway," she said. "Well, the thing is, um, Becker Cain is really bad news, and I think we need to do something about the situation."

Just as Lauren had expected, a look of surprise crossed each face. Everyone sat silently for what seemed like ages.

Finally Brooks spoke up. "Lauren," he said in an embarrassed voice. "I don't like Becker either, but if Faith is happy with him, we don't have any right to interfere in her life."

Winnie nodded in agreement. "We've made a big enough mess of our friendships with Faith. She likes this Becker guy. Trying to break up her romance would be the worst thing we could do."

"Can I say something here?" Josh scratched his arm through a rip in the sleeve of his T-shirt. "Lauren, we all know you're really into this feminism thing and that's cool. But not every male is the enemy. You may not like Becker, but that doesn't mean he's bad news. You know how kind of carried away and . . . uh . . . violent you can get."

Lauren swallowed her pride. She had seen this one coming, and she deserved it. Not long ago, at the peak of her enthusiasm for feminism and self-defense, she'd had an embarrassing incident with Becker. After an argument with Melissa, she had gone to Faith's room to sleep. She'd forgotten about Coed-by-Bed, and the fact that Becker was staying there temporarily instead of Liza. When Becker came home, Lauren had mistaken him for an intruder and beaten him up pretty badly before she realized who he was.

"I know I went overboard on the self-defense stuff," Lauren responded. "I know I was out of line when I attacked Becker. But I'm still right about him. I wish I weren't, but I am. Has anybody ever heard of SPEAR?"

Cody nodded. "Sure. I did a radio piece on it last

year. It's sort of like a cult. The guru is some guy named Tom Spearman. He's really into mind-control and stuff like that. It's not religious though. It's about success, right? And his followers are mostly well-off college kids and even some high-school students. They take seminars to learn his weird make-your-own-rules philosophy."

Lauren bit her lip. "Guess what, gang? Becker Cain was a member when he was in his senior year at Wellington High, in California. He took a bunch of seminars and he even ran away from home for a while to live with the group."

"You're kidding!" Winnie's eyes widened and she nervously twisted the three scarves that she wore around her waist for a belt. "This does not sound good."

Lauren nodded. "Anyway, Becker was really into it until his parents pulled him out of it. But I think he's still a follower—you know, go after what you want, don't worry about the rules."

"He's probably changed since high school," Winnie reasoned. "We all have—at least I hope we have. Maybe he's okay now. Maybe it's not a big deal."

"There's more," Lauren said. "I've always had a weird feeling about him, so I asked around. There's a girl in my writing lab—a smart, pretty girl named Jessica. She was involved with Becker last fall. She really liked him for a while. She said he was incredibly attentive and into anything she wanted. She said he was pretty sexy, too."

Brooks turned pale.

Lauren took a breath. "Jessica is a writer, of course, and she really wanted to get into this special writing workshop they held over Christmas break. So Becker kept telling her he was going to help her achieve her dreams. And he did—by forging a letter of recommendation."

"Oh, no!" Josh breathed, looking around the circle.

"Oh, yes," Lauren informed. "The forgery was discovered and the girl got kicked out of the workshop on the first day. She was totally humiliated and she's on academic probation now because of it."

"Are you sure she's telling the truth?" Cody asked gently, straightening the suede vest he wore over his work shirt. "You're a journalist. I'm a DJ. We've both seen cases where somebody tries to get back at an old boyfriend or girlfriend."

"Jessica showed me the letter from the Dean," Lauren replied. "And the only reason she told me was because she knew I was concerned about Faith. Jessica isn't looking for publicity. In fact, she said if I wrote anything about it in the newspaper, she'd deny the whole thing."

There was a long silence as everyone digested Lauren's troubling news.

"Maybe I should drop by and have a little chat with

the guy," Brooks offered. "You know, just let him know that there are people who care a lot about Faith and wouldn't want to see her hurt." He flexed his wrist and rubbed it with his other hand.

"You mean bully him into backing off? Loom over him and threaten violence? That route never works." Lauren's voice was flat and totally deadpan. She waited a beat, then lifted one humorous eyebrow. "Besides, I already tried it."

After a moment of stunned silence, everybody burst into hysterical laughter. Winnie threw her arms around Lauren and rested the top of her spiky hairdo on her shoulder. "Poor Lauren," she chuckled.

"Poor Becker," Cody managed to say, making them laugh even harder.

When things finally calmed down, Brooks spoke up. "That's not what I meant," he protested.

Winnie's expression turned serious. "Then what exactly did you mean?"

"I just . . ." Brooks broke off in helpless confusion. Then he smiled sheepishly. "I guess that is what I meant. Sorry. I just couldn't think of anything else to do. And I can't stand the thought of anybody hurting Faith."

Cody turned to Lauren. "What if you just lay it out for Faith the way you laid it out for us?" he asked. "Tell her what you told us and then let her work it out for herself."

Winnie pulled a whistle from around her neck and blew it. "Hold it. Stop. Negative. Time out," she said, waving her arms like a referee. The charm bracelets she wore on her arm jangled. "Take it from me, psych major and daughter of a psychologist. You confront Faith directly and she'll just defend Becker. She wants to believe in him. The harder you try to convince her he's bad news, the more she'll work to prove you wrong."

"She's right," KC said. "And if we try to separate her from Becker, she'll think it's because we want her back in the old role: good old Faith, always ready to put her own problems aside to help us with ours."

"Yo. What if we showed her that we're all doing really well and have our lives under control?" Winnie suggested. "Make it clear that we want her back as our friend, not our chief problem-solver and bottle-washer."

"How would we do that?" Lauren asked.

"A party!" Winnie fell back against Josh and plucked happily at his shirt. "I've been saying party for some time here. Josh and I can have it at our house. I'll prove I can be a responsible grown-up for once and take care of everything."

"Oh, yeah?" Josh teased.

Winnie whacked him playfully. "When Faith comes over, we'll all be there—getting along great with each other like civilized adults. Then, when it feels right, we can apologize to her for acting like a bunch of brats. We can tell her that we want her back in our lives, you know, and show her that she can lean on us for a change if she feels like it. Then she won't feel like she has to hold on so tightly to Becker."

Lauren laughed. "You know, that's not a bad idea."

"I know," Winnie beamed.

"I like it," KC confirmed with a brisk nod of her head.

"I'll make it très terrific," Winnie said. "A brunch at noon on Saturday. Purple napkins folded up like Japanese birds. Sushi, cheesy mushrooms, pesto pizza, and those animal cookies with the icing—you know, the kind we had when we were five. The whole nine yards. It'll be a kind of reunion. We haven't had a party with everybody in a long time."

Lauren cleared her throat timidly. "What would everybody think about asking Melissa? I know she'll be busy getting ready for the Olympic trials. I guess her meet is even that same afternoon. But maybe she would stop by on her way, so we could wish her luck. I think she'd like to know that we all care."

Every pair of eyes turned toward Brooks. He blushed furiously and looked at his muddy hiking boots.

"I think that's a great idea," Winnie said, breaking the awkward silence. "We've tried to be friends with her lately and she's kind of pushed us away. But why not try again? I say, if at first you don't succeed, try about five thousand more times."

"I'll second that," KC said. "I think she saw us at the meet yesterday, and I think she was glad we were there."

"Brooks?" Lauren prompted. She hadn't wanted to embarrass him, but at some point, if he was going to have to face Melissa, he should at least express his opinion.

Brooks lifted his head and nodded slowly. "Sure." He sighed loudly. Then he looked back at Lauren. "Maybe we should invite Dash, too."

Lauren felt her cheeks flush and everyone began to laugh. Everyone except Brooks, that is, who merely smiled and nodded as if he were just trying to go along with the gang.

"He got you," Winnie crowed. "Now you're it."

Lauren and Brooks exchanged a look. His face looked strained. She knew that her cheeks were hot.

"Okay," Lauren said. "Here's the deal. I'll be responsible for inviting Faith and Melissa, as long as someone else invites Dash."

"I'll do that," Brooks agreed.

Lauren looked out over the pond again and felt that something very important had been decided. She smiled at her circle of friends. She pushed thoughts of Dash out of her mind and concentrated on Faith. If all went well at the party, Faith would be back. Their circle would soon be complete again, and stronger than ever.

# Four

fffftttt.

Brooks threw a flat rock out over the surface of Mill Pond.

"At least I can still skip rocks," he muttered. "At least I'm still sure about how to do that."

He sat alone watching the last few canoes paddle across the calm surface of the water. The meeting had broken up. Cody had left to walk KC over to her sorority house. Lauren had gone to the library. Winnie had gone to volunteer at the Crisis Hot Line and Josh had headed over to the computer center.

Everybody else had been in a great mood by the end of the get-together. Brooks had tried to look happy about everything and participate in the plans, but he was feeling confused and depressed. He really didn't see the point of this party business. If the girls thought it was worth trying, he was game, but the Becker thing sounded pretty ominous.

What sounded more deadly, though, was having Melissa there. Suppose she came to the party? What then? How was he supposed to act?

He really didn't know. All he knew was that lately he'd rather walk naked through a pit of rattlesnakes than face her. The thought of it made his stomach muscles clench.

On the opposite bank of the pond, two girls in shorts and heavy sweaters tossed a Frisbee. A large black terrier happily leaped high in the air and caught it in his mouth. The girls converged on the dog, patting him and cheering. He sighed and suddenly understood the expression *lucky dog.*

Brooks bent his head and rested it wearily on his thick forearms. How did life get so complicated? he wondered. He'd come to college feeling like he had his whole life under control, knowing exactly what was expected of him. Now, he didn't feel in control of anything. And he sure didn't know what was expected of him. All he knew was that he'd felt lousy for a long time. Ever since he'd jilted Melissa, to be exact.

"God," he moaned.

He still couldn't believe he had done it. Couldn't believe that he, Brooks Baldwin—a gentleman, scholar, athlete, and all-around stand-up guy—had utterly humiliated someone he cared very much about.

"Hey, man. You okay? You look like you just lost your last friend."

Brooks lifted his head and saw Dash Ramirez hop out of a canoe onto the shore. He wore a red bandanna tied over his dark hair and a dark green T-shirt. His eyes were brown and intense. He wasn't a big guy, like Brooks, but he had that kind of wiry build that was stronger than it looked.

"I'll live. How 'bout you?" Brooks asked.

Dash shrugged and pulled the canoe up on the bank. "I've been better. I've been hiding out on the water behind a tree. I was sitting there so long I thought a bird might build a nest on my head."

Brooks looked puzzled.

"I saw your powwow up here," Dash explained. "I was going to stop by, but I was afraid Lauren might rough me up."

Brooks laughed. "Oh, no. Lauren doesn't believe in problem-solving through violence."

"That's not what I hear." Dash pulled the bandanna off his head.

Brooks smiled. "Well, she says she's changed."

"You ever notice how women are allowed to go

through these changes?" Dash commented wryly. "But we're just male chauvinist pigs from the womb to the tomb." He sat down on the dock next to Brooks. "So what was the big meeting about?"

Brooks stared at Dash for a minute, watching him fold the bandanna again and retie it on his head. He liked Dash. Dash was a really good reporter. He acted streetwise and cynical, but Brooks knew it was partly an act. It was the way a lot of guys acted when their feelings had been diced into tiny pieces by a woman.

Brooks threw another rock across the water. "I'm not sure. You know that T-shirt that Lauren used to wear? The one that said *Men! They just don't get it*. Well, that T-shirt was right. I don't get it. I'm *trying* to get it. Faith is mad at everybody and Becker Cain is bad news. We're all going to have a party and look like we have our stuff together now. Then at the end of the party, we'll all be friends again. By the way, you're invited."

Dash let out a little sigh.

Brooks frowned at Dash. "Do *you* get it?"

Dash's mouth fell open and he stared back at Brooks for a moment. Then he threw back his head and began to laugh.

And then Brooks began to laugh, too. He kicked the muddy heel of his boot against the ground. It was nice to be with another guy, one who didn't have a girlfriend and wasn't an outdoor-type or a jock—

like the guys in his dorm. This sure wasn't the kind of stuff he could laugh about with his soccer or hiking friends.

"Sounds like you need the Men's Support Group—bad," Dash finally managed to choke.

"The what?"

Dash went over and fished his backpack out of the canoe. He pulled the latest issue of the *U of S Weekly Journal* out of the pack and handed it to Brooks. "Page five. Third column from the right," he said, flopping down again.

Brooks opened the paper and immediately saw the column that Dash was talking about. Two paragraphs announced the formation of the U of S Men's Support Group for men who felt "confused or alienated by the opposite sex."

"That's me," Brooks confirmed. "Because I am totally confused and alienated by the opposite sex."

"You and me both," Dash admitted. "So tell me more about the party." Dash stretched his legs out in front of him.

But Brooks was reading the rest of the article. The group was going to meet once a week on Wednesdays to talk about the problems of male/female relations. The article said there was a sign up sheet in the Student Union. Maybe it was a way to start feeling better about things and quit feeling guilty all the time, he decided. "Tell me more about this group," Brooks responded. "I might be interested."

Dash snatched the paper away. "I was kidding about this. Stuff like that usually turns out to be a waste of time. You can't solve real problems with a lot of chitchat. Tell me more about the party."

"Saturday at Winnie's. You should come. It's supposed to be a reunion party. Lauren's going to be there. Maybe you two could get back together."

Dash bit his lip and stared out over the water. "I think it's going to take more than a party to get Lauren and me back together."

"What would it take?"

Dash shook his head.

"So what would it take?" Brooks asked again.

"I wish I knew." Dash scratched the dark stubble on his chin. "If I knew, I'd do something about it. But I don't know how to communicate with her anymore. Everything I do makes things worse. Everything I say makes her angry."

"You know what your problem is?"

"What?"

"You don't read your own newspaper."

Brooks took the newspaper back and tapped his finger against the page. "Look at the topic for the first Men's Support Group meeting. 'What Do Women Want?'"

Dash took the paper, read it, then stared dolefully

out over the water. "The guy who finally figures that out ought to get the Nobel Prize for peace."

Something about Dash's face made Brooks feel even more depressed. Maybe it was because Dash looked like Brooks felt. Whipped. Defeated. Hurt. And *helpless.*

Brooks stood and dusted the seat of his jeans. "I don't know about you, but on Wednesday I'm going to check it out."

"You're kidding."

Brooks grinned. "Nope."

"You're *really* going, man?"

"I'm *really* going. I'm going over there right now to put my name on the sign-up sheet."

Brooks shoved his hands in his pockets and began walking away. Just knowing he was taking some action made him feel better already. It might be foolish. It might be nutty. But he hated feeling so confused, so angry, and so guilty about it. Hurting girls who had never done him any harm. Having girls hurt him. He was only a freshman, for God's sake, and he was already among the walking wounded.

"Hey, Brooks."

Brooks kept walking.

"Come on, Baldwin. Wait up!"

Brooks turned and saw Dash hoist the canoe and balance it on his head.

"What?"

"I'm going too."

"You're not *really* going?" Brooks grinned.

"I'm *really* going," Dash answered.

"Why?"

"I'm going to get the scoop of the century."

"Oh yeah?"

Dash laughed. "I'm going to find out what women want."

# Five

ey! It's not an exact science. I don't *know* what it does. Why don't you just try it? Then you can tell me."

There was no mistaking the anger in the body-builder's voice. His name was Greg. He weighed a hulking two-seventy-five and had a flat top. Bodybuilders were the chief users and sellers of steroids on campus, but half the time even they weren't sure what they were buying or selling.

Melissa hesitated. The stuff was expensive. What if it didn't work? The 'roid dungeon was colder than usual in the early evenings, and Melissa could feel the chilly concrete through the thick soles of her running shoes. Usually Caitlin made the buys, but Caitlin had evening classes on Mondays, which was why Melissa was taking care of it this time. Their supply was low and the girls had agreed to double their medication between now and the trials on Saturday, hoping it would double their chances of winning.

Greg narrowed his eyes angrily. "Make up your mind. If you don't want to buy it, somebody else will. It's a gamble, McDormand, but it's your choice. Do you want the stuff or not?"

Melissa's heart began to beat uncomfortably fast. She noticed that Greg's eyes looked yellow. Yellow-tinged eyes indicated heavy steroid use, and she had heard of 'roid rages, the sudden outbursts of violent temper that steroids could produce. There was nobody else in the dungeon and Greg was getting increasingly antagonistic. She took a cautious step back and lifted her hands up, palms out. "Okay. Okay," she said, hoping to make peace. "Don't get excited." Her muscles were tensed and ready to run if she had to.

Greg's angry face relented. "Sorry. Sometimes I get a little hostile. Nothing personal. It's just the 'roids." Then he began to laugh. "Ever happen to you?"

Melissa laughed, too. But mainly out of nervous relief. "No. I've always had a little problem with my temper, but so far, no 'roid rages. Though you may see me have one on Saturday if I don't win."

He flashed her a crooked grin. "Something to look forward to," he joked.

Melissa smiled. What she was looking forward to was another important win. She remembered how in all her classes today, she'd received a round of applause when she had walked into the room. And during this afternoon's series of practice runs, Coach Terry had treated her like a princess. Yesterday's win was turning her whole life around. "I'll buy," she said confidently.

"All right!" Greg said. "You want some right now?"

Melissa nodded. The sooner she started medicating, the better. Saturday wasn't that far away.

Greg reached into his gym bag and pulled out a disposable syringe. He quickly filled it. "You want me to do the honors?"

Melissa laughed and took the syringe. "No thanks."

Greg put his hands over his eyes while Melissa lowered her shorts, twisted around, and punched the needle into the fleshy part on the back of her hip.

"Done," she said. Then she gasped as her heart gave a hard thump two seconds after she removed the needle. It was definitely working. Pumping through her system like rocket fuel. "Wow!" she breathed. "This stuff is incredible."

Greg reached into his gym bag and took out some vials. "I'll say. This may have something else in it, too. Who knows, and who cares, right? It gets the job done."

Melissa dug down into the pocket of her jacket for her money. By the time they had completed the transaction, Melissa felt like Superwoman. She caught a glimpse of herself in the cracked mirror on the wall and smiled. She looked like Superwoman, too. Her legs had always had a nice shape, but the added calf definition and thigh development she'd gotten with the drugs gave them a sexy and powerful look. Sure, her freckled skin didn't look as perfect as it used to, but she didn't have the broken-out look that came with using. As soon as she'd noticed the first break-out, she'd hit the tanning beds, and she was darker than she'd ever been in her life. She figured that her green eyes almost glowed in the dark now.

"Race you up the stairs?" Greg offered as they left the dungeon.

"Last one to the top is a ninety-pound weakling," Melissa shouted, starting up the stairs at a run with her gym bag in her hand. Halfway up the second flight, she felt a tiny twinge in her right Achilles tendon and yipped.

"You hurt something?" Greg panted as he ran behind her. "Want to sit down and rest?"

Melissa shook her head and started climbing again. Greg was panting, but Melissa wasn't even winded. And right now, she was so pumped she couldn't rest if her life depended on it. "I'd have to be in a lot more pain than that to rest."

"Right on." Greg laughed. "Pain is for wimps."

"Pain is for wimps," Melissa agreed as she planted her foot on the top step of the last flight of stairs.

Greg slapped her on the back and she pushed open the door. They both broke into conspiratorial giggles as they hurried out into the hall and headed for the weight room.

CLANK! CLANK! CLANK!

Every plate in the weight room seemed to be moving when they walked in. It was crowded this evening. Full of runners, football players, bodybuilders, and basketball jocks. "I'm going to start with squats," Greg said. "See you later."

Melissa nodded and hurried across the room toward one of the few vacant lifting benches. She took off her warmup jacket, stuffed it in her gym bag, and stowed it under the bench. Her nostrils flared with pleasure as she sat down and inhaled the smell in the weight room—a combination of leather, witch hazel, and the clean bleachy smell of the rough white gym towels.

The lifting benches were scattered around the perimeter of the room, tucked between weight racks and machines. In a row against the mirror lay dumbbells of varying size and weight.

There were two guys spotting each other at the central squat rack. Melissa watched them grunt and strain as she stretched her arms high over her head.

She leaned over and picked up a ten-pound dumb-bell in each hand. The 'roids were really pumping and she quickly worked her way through three sets of ten repetitions. She dropped the dumbbells to the floor and lifted her arms to stretch. Ten pounds had been too easy. Maybe she should try a few more reps with fifteen pounds in each hand.

She leaned forward. But just before her hand closed over the fifteen-pound dumbbell, something strange happened. All of a sudden, Melissa felt the hair on her arms stand up. *Somebody is watching me.* Her heart began to beat faster and she felt almost afraid.

Melissa snapped her head to the left, but all she saw was a football player whose eyes were intent on the stack of weights that were moving up and down on the leg press with a loud *clank, clank, clank.*

She looked to her right. A sprinter from the men's track team chinned himself on a bar.

Maybe the meds were making her paranoid, she decided. She leaned forward again . . . and then she saw a pair of green eyes staring at her from the other side of the weight room. A little thrill of electricity raced through her body. She wasn't crazy. Somebody *was* watching her.

Half of him was hidden by the pulleys and scaffold-ing of the multiuse rack. But she could see the heavily muscled upper torso that flared out from his narrow waist. Wide chest. Powerful shoulders. He wore a yellow tank top that said *Feet Don't Fail Me Now*, and a sweatband that held back golden blond hair. Both of his hands were encased in fingerless leather gloves.

Melissa didn't mean to stare, but he literally took her breath away. He was almost as tan as she. His mouth was full and slightly turned up into a smile. Even from across the gym she could see that his eyes, like hers, were very green.

*He's staring back at me,* she realized.

His smile grew bigger, and for some reason Melissa sensed a challenge. Without taking his eyes off of her, he leaned slightly forward and began to curl a dumbbell, bringing the weight to his chest in a smooth, motion. He was curling a lot of weight. And he was daring her to do the same.

Melissa smiled back and felt her body come alive with excitement. *You're on.* She reached for a bigger dumbbell, determined to match him curl for curl.

He paused for a moment as she shifted her position and planted her feet more comfortably. She gave him a little nod, telling him she was ready, and he curled again. Melissa lifted her dumbbell toward her chest, trying to sync her movement with his.

When he lowered the weight, so did she. But she was a little too fast and her dumbbell reached the bottom of the arc before his. *Darn!* Curling the

dumbbell up to the chest was actually easier than trying to control the weight on the way down. It took a
lot of muscle control to lower it slowly.

He pointed with his eyes toward the discarded
fifteen-pound dumbbell that lay at her feet. The meaning of the look was clear. He was telling her that he'd
noticed her difficulty, and he was offering her the
chance to switch back to the lighter-weight dumbbell.

No way! Melissa bit her lip so she wouldn't burst
out laughing. When she got control of herself, she lifted her chin haughtily and gripped her weight again.

His green eyes flashed with amusement and pointed again to the fifteen-pound dumbbell. *Don't be
stubborn,* the look said.

She pursed her lips and narrowed her eyes in a parody
of a glare. *Don't do me any favors,* said her return look.

He rolled his eyes. *Have it your way.*

A snort of laughter escaped her. She looked back at him,
then forced her face into a mask of grim determination.

His eyes locked on hers again, and they worked out
together. They lifted and lowered, lifted and lowered.
His full lips curved into an intimate smile, and
Melissa felt herself grow warmer and a little breathless. It was like a dance. A slow, incredibly romantic
dance, although in reality they'd never even exchanged
a word or a touch.

Finally, he broke the eye contact and leaned down

to pick up an even larger weight. Then he shot her a look that said, *More?*

BONK!

She let the dumbbell drop to the floor and held up her hands in surrender.

He laughed and winked at her. Then he lowered his eyes to the dumbbell in his hand. Melissa felt him withdraw his attention and turn it back inward as he continued with his own regimen. The dance was over, and she was disappointed.

*Come back*, she wanted to scream.

Sweat streamed down her neck and back and Melissa toweled off. Usually she was standoffish with guys, but maybe the steroids had made her bold. She strode over to the squat rack. She didn't know if it was the 'roids or the admiration she'd seen in his eyes, but she felt as if she could lift a thousand pounds. She piled the iron plates onto the bar. She knew she should warm up first, but didn't want to bother. She was determined to get his attention again.

Melissa jostled plates so that they made a nice CLANK.

It worked. He was staring at her again, just his upper body visible over the rack.

Melissa positioned her body under the bar. She closed her eyes and shifted the weight onto her shoulders, feeling the strain on her leg muscles.

When she bent her knees, she felt a pain in her right Achilles tendon. *Pain is for wimps! Pain is for wimps!* she thought, refusing to give in and stop.

She lifted again and the pain got worse, bunching up around the back of her ankle like a nest of hot coals. Melissa gritted her teeth and bent her knees, again and again, working through the pain and lifting until she felt like she could safely quit without losing face.

Finally, she replaced the weight on the rack. "Wheeeew!" she breathed heavily.

She opened her eyes and was happy to see that he was watching her intently from the other side of the room. But if he was so interested, why hadn't he come over to join her for a lower-body workout? Maybe he wasn't as interested as she thought.

Finding courage, Melissa grabbed her towel and started over to his side of the room. The rowing machine was on that side of the room. She'd pretend she wanted to do some rowing, and that would give him a chance to speak to her if he felt like it.

Forcing herself not to limp, Melissa crossed the room. When she came around the center weight rack, she stopped. There was a metal chair sitting next to the bench, a wheelchair. Melissa looked around the gym, searching for the person who the metal chair belonged to.

Then something yellow flickered in the corner of

her eye and she turned her head just in time to see the blond guy again. He pulled the wheelchair over until it was right next to his knees, then reached over and flipped the brakes on.

Melissa felt the bottom of her jaw drop. She realized with a shock that it was *his* wheelchair. There were no arms on the chair and the aluminum wheels looked like the wheels of a racing bike. He positioned his strong arms on the lifting bench where he sat, then pushed off, balancing the weight of his entire body on his arms, and gracefully pivoting his lower torso into the black leather seat of the chair.

*Don't stare, idiot!* her brain yelled. But as hard as she tried, she simply couldn't drag her eyes away. He was wearing bulky gray sweatpants, but now she could see that the legs underneath were thin. Quickly and efficiently, he picked up his legs and positioned them so that his feet rested side-by-side on the parallel foot pedals. His lower torso didn't move, but the upper part of his body leaned down and picked up a canvas gym bag which he settled in his lap.

She was still watching him with a gaping mouth when he looked up and caught her staring. His eyes held hers and for a split second, she saw the same defiant look in his eyes that she had seen so often in her own mirror.

Melissa flushed with embarrassment and felt

ashamed of herself. She understood what that look meant. It meant he didn't appreciate being the object of her curiosity—or pity. But still she couldn't look away.

His eyelids fluttered down and she noticed that his lashes were thick and golden, just like his hair. When he lifted his eyes again, he flashed her a crooked grin. "I beat you on the biceps," he said in a deep voice. "But I guess you win on the leg squats."

A sheen of perspiration on his golden skin caught the light and threw the perfectly formed muscles of his arms and shoulders into high relief. Melissa's lips moved, trying to form a response, but then her eyes took in the wheelchair again, and her mind went blank.

"Let's do this again soon," he said with a wink. Then his powerful arms went into action, sending the chair speeding across the gym and out the door.

The last thing Melissa saw was I BRAKE FOR PEDESTRIANS, the bumper sticker pasted on the leather back of the chair.

Melissa's eye lingered on the door long after he was gone, and she wished with all her might that she'd been able to think of something to say.

# Six

"How about George Washington Gaffey?" Josh suggested. He turned the page of his American history textbook. "Ulysses S. Grant Gaffey? Or do you think Nathan Hale Gaffey might be a good name?"

Winnie laughed and flopped back against the bright cushions and red afghan that covered their threadbare living-room sofa. "It might be a girl, you know." She shifted her back a little and adjusted a pillow behind it. There was still only the tiniest bulge below her waist. But for the last few days, her hips and lower back had ached at night.

"Good point," Josh said, flipping the pages. "Give

me a minute and let me get back to you on that one."
His slender frame slumped down and his big blue eyes
scanned up and down a page of his textbook.

Winnie smothered a yawn and wondered if being
pregnant was affecting her mind as well as her back.
Having a party on Saturday had seemed like a great
idea that afternoon at Mill Pond. But now, at eight
o'clock at night, it seemed like a pretty overwhelming
proposition. Their high-ceilinged living room looked
like a yard sale upset by a hurricane. Winnie's clothes
and school books littered the floor, along with boxes
of Josh's computer equipment, as well as the junk left
by their two housemates, Clifford and Rich. Papers
and clothing were piled high on two of the wing
chairs—both of which were losing their stuffing
through holes in the back. And junk galore was piled
on and around and under the ring-stained coffee table
in front of the sofa. It was going to be a lot of work
to get the place ready for a party by Saturday.

"Okay. Take your pick," Josh said, interrupting her
thoughts. "Dolly Madison Gaffey? Harriet Tubman
Gaffey? Or Betsy Ross Gaffey?"

Winnie grabbed Josh's American history book
from his hand and threw it behind the sofa. "Enough
with the American heroes series. It's a baby, Josh, not
a Franklin Mint collectable."

"Hey!" Josh protested. "I had a very efficient system

worked out here for doing two things at once—
studying for my American history exam and naming
the baby."

"I know," Winnie giggled. "But I don't want you
to be so efficient. It makes me feel like I have to do
two things at once. And I don't want to do anything
right now. I just want to be a blob, an ever-growing,
changing blob of protoplasm." Winnie leaned into
the curve of his shoulder. She felt Josh's arm tighten
around her and she snuggled even deeper.

It was wonderful having some quiet time alone with
her husband. Not that she didn't like Rich and
Clifford. They were both great guys. Rich, with his
ventriloquist's dummy, was always making her laugh.
And Clifford, who was a stuffy science major, was
funny without knowing he was funny.

But it was nice to have the big, slightly tattered,
four-bedroom Victorian house to themselves for
awhile. Rich spent most of his time these days hanging out in amateur comedy clubs. And Clifford was
holed up in the library studying for a big science
exam. Oops! That was another thing she'd have to
take care of before the party, Winnie realized. There
were four crates of Clifford's weird science stuff
stacked in the dining alcove off the kitchen. She'd
have to remember to ask him to move them.

Winnie buried her face in Josh's shoulder and

groaned. "I'm just beginning to realize there's going to be a ton of stuff to do to get ready for the party."

"Two tons," Josh agreed, resting his head against the back of the sofa. "I didn't want to say anything, but it struck me this afternoon that this party might not be the greatest idea in the world. We've both got a lot of school work. I'm going to be pulling a lot of all-nighters in the computer lab this week. And you get tired pretty easily these days."

"Why didn't you stop me?" Winnie said mournfully. "You know I forget to engage brain before opening mouth sometimes."

"Because I didn't have a gag," he laughed. "That's the only thing I can think of that would stop you from doing something crazy once you've made up your mind to do it."

She reached under his T-shirt and pinched the skin of his waist.

"Cut it out," he giggled.

"Oh, well," Winnie chirped. "It's for a good cause. I really strung Faith out when I got her all involved in that last fight you and I had. The least I can do to make it up to her is organize a party."

"Forget the party for now," Josh said with a grin. "Let's think about the baby. How about Mick Jagger Gaffey? Or Annie Lennox Gaffey? Bruce Springsteen Gaffey? Wolfgang Amadeus Mozart Gaffey?"

"What are you doing now?" Winnie giggled, happy to forget about the party for the present. "Studying for your music history exam?"

Josh extricated his arm from beneath Winnie's head. Then he jumped up, grabbed his boom box from the mantle, and came back to the sofa. "Let's see how Baby Gaffey feels about music."

He tuned the radio softly to the rock and roll station and pressed the speaker against Winnie's stomach. Then he opened Winnie's mouth and spoke into her throat, as if shouting down a well. "Hello, down there. Can you hear me?"

Winnie laughed. But since Josh was holding her mouth open, it came out more like a gargle in the back of her throat. "Josh, it's still only about the size of a fingernail."

"I don't care. Hello!" Josh called again. Then he pretended to listen. "No, this is *not* a sales call," he yelped indignantly. "This is your father speaking. My name is Josh Gaffey."

He pretended to listen again. "Nice to meet you, too."

Josh looked at Winnie and grinned. "Good manners. Must get that from your side of the family." He leaned forward and listened at Winnie's throat. "What? Oh, sure. No problem."

He gently closed Winnie's mouth and began

changing the radio station until it played soft symphonic music. "He says he prefers classical."

Winnie grabbed Josh. "You are my adorable, snugly, computer-nerd husband, and I love you."

"I love you, too," Josh responded.

No hesitation. No mumbling. No qualifying. Just a flat out declaration of love. *What more could I ask for?* Winnie thought happily. At first, she'd feared that her pregnancy was going to drive them apart. But now that Josh had gotten over the initial shock, it was bringing them closer every day. Sure, it was forcing them to change and to grow, but that was good. At least that's what her mom would say.

Thinking about her mother produced a little twinge of guilt and she groaned.

"Are you okay?" Josh asked.

"Yeah. I'm just thinking about how I really need to tell Mom about the baby. After all, if she's going to be a grandmother, she might like a little time to get used to the idea."

Josh nodded. Without hesitating, he picked up the phone, which sat on a pedestal table next to the sofa. "She's at her office on Monday nights, right? Let's call her right now." He laughed, beginning to dial the number. "Share the good news."

"Wait!"

Josh's finger hovered over the dialing pad. "Problem?"

Winnie sat up and ran her hand through her hair, spiking up the top like she always did when she was nervous. "I'm not sure I'm in the mood to be shrink-rapped right now."

"Shrink-rapped?"

"My mom's *shrink-rap* goes something like this. . . . First, she listens. Then she clears her throat and goes totally neutral and unemotional . . . like she's a Vulcan or something. After that, she delivers the old *you're a grown-up now and it's not up to me to validate your decisions* speech."

"She's right. You *are* a grown-up."

"I know. But I want her to validate my decisions anyway."

"Then give her a chance," Josh said, dialing the number.

He listened. Then, "Hello? Yes, could you tell me, does Dr. Gottlieb validate?"

Winnie began to laugh.

Josh turned to Winnie. "Her secretary says there's free parking across the street."

"Give me that!" Winnie dove across his lap and snatched the phone from Josh's hand. "Hello, Doris? This is Winnie. Can I speak to my mom?"

"I should have known!" Her mother's secretary laughed. "Hang on and I'll put you through."

Winnie waited, her heart beginning to pound.

Suddenly, the picture of her permissive yet distant mother vanished and Winnie's memory ran a mental montage of her high-school years. She remembered her mother dancing away in the living room with Faith and KC at Winnie's sixteenth birthday party. She remembered her mom with a mouth full of pins, helping Winnie put together the most outrageous prom dress the world had ever seen. She closed her eyes and saw her mom screaming and shouting with glee over Winnie's acceptance letter to the University of Springfield.

A lump rose in Winnie's throat. Of course her mother was going to be thrilled. And once she'd finished the shrink-rap, she'd be full of plans and suggestions and enthusiasm.

There was a click. "Hi, honey!"

"I've got big news," Winnie said, practically choking on her words. "Wonderful, fabulous, earth-shaking news."

Her mom sounded rushed. "That's great, Win, and I want to hear all about it. But I'm about to begin a counseling session. Can it keep until Thursday?"

"Thursday?" Winnie echoed.

"I'm coming to Springfield on Thursday. So I'll see you in person. I've got a few things to do, and I'll be in the area through Sunday." She heard her mother turn her mouth away from the phone and mumble something.

"Mom?"

"Winnie! I really need to get into my session. Listen, I've got a lot to do between now and then so I won't call you back. Just look for me sometime Thursday morning. Okay? I can't wait to see you. Love to Josh. Bye."

Click. The line went dead.

"Well?" Josh asked. "What happened?"

"She's coming to Springfield for a few days on Thursday morning," Winnie said brightly. "I'll get to tell her in person." She brightened even more as a second thought hit her. "She'll be here for the party. And you know what? Once Mom hears the news, she's going to want to party in a big way."

Winnie settled into Josh's lap and positioned her aching back comfortably against his warm stomach. This was working out great. Her mother was a good planner and an even better organizer. She'd get the house straightened up in no time. Then she'd whisk down to the store and whip up nine different kinds of party food in less than an hour. She'd probably even figure out some way to turn the event into a reunion and an impromptu baby shower rolled into one.

Suddenly, Winnie stopped feeling overwhelmed. Her mom was coming, and she'd take care of everything.

# Seven

Lauren paused uncertainly in the hallway of Coleridge Hall. She had decided to wait until now to invite Faith to the party because she was pretty sure Faith would be in her room at ten o'clock at night. But now that she was here, she wondered if she'd made a mistake. Maybe it was too late to drop in. She turned and began to walk back to the steps that led to the lobby. On the other hand . . . Lauren pivoted on the heel of her boot and started back toward Faith's room. It was important to invite Faith as soon as possible before she made other plans for Saturday.

Lauren lifted her fist to knock on Faith's door, then

hesitated. *What if she's asleep? What if she's in the middle of something important? What if she doesn't want to see me?*

Lauren threw back her shoulders and adjusted her wire-rimmed glasses. This was ridiculous. She was letting her old, horrible insecurities keep her from getting her dearest friend back. *Just knock on her door. Smile. And invite her to the party. What's the worst that can happen?* She lifted her fist again and knocked softly.

No answer. Lauren timidly pressed her ear against the door and heard the radio playing.

She knocked again. "Faith?"

There was a creak and the sound of footsteps padding softly across the floor. The door opened a crack and one pale blue eye stared out.

Lauren's mouth fell open in surprise. "Becker!" She felt her cheeks growing pink. The worst thing that could happen was that Becker could be here.

He opened the door a little wider and Lauren's eyes took in the lean body, the long dark hair, and the loose white shirt that reminded her of a monk. *Why does bad news have to be so attractive,* she thought sourly. Winnie's party was going to have to be a real humdinger to get Faith's mind off of this guy. Still, no sense in antagonizing Becker. She shoved her hands down into the pockets of her parachute pants and forced a conciliatory smile on her face.

"Hi," she said in the friendliest voice she could manage. "Is Faith here?"

Becker's mouth curved into a smile even more conciliatory than hers. "No. She's out. I'm sorry." He kept smiling, but he didn't say anything else. Obviously, he wasn't prepared to tell Lauren where Faith was. Oh well, she didn't blame him. The last time they'd met, she had jumped him in the dark and beaten him up. He probably thought she was a nut. *Look who's talking?* her mind immediately responded. If anybody was a nut, it was Becker.

"Is Liza here?" she asked. Maybe Faith's brassy roommate would know where Lauren could find her.

"I haven't seen Liza all day," Becker said.

Lauren remembered running into Liza a few days ago. Liza had said she wasn't spending much time in her room these days because she was busy rehearsing for some study project for her acting class.

Becker wrinkled his brow, trying to look like he was sorry to be so unhelpful. But Lauren had a feeling he was enjoying this. There was just something so smug about his smile. She'd been embarrassed at first. But now she was getting angry.

"If neither Faith nor Liza is in, what are you doing here?" she asked bluntly.

"I have my own key," he said in a matter-of-fact tone. "And Faith has a key to my room. We're very close." His voice was kind and patient and unbearably patronizing.

Lauren gritted her teeth, determined not to lose her temper. "Would you give Faith a message?" she asked. "Would you please tell her that Winnie is having a party on Saturday and she'd like Faith to come? The party starts at noon. If Faith is thinking about going to the Olympic trials on Saturday, the event is sold out already, but we'll all watch the meet on television at the party."

"Faith and I want to spend our weekend alone together," Becker responded. "But thank you for asking us," he added. "We'll be there if we can."

Becker started to shut the door and Lauren instinctively jumped forward and wedged her shoulder between the door and the jamb. He recoiled a little and Lauren blushed furiously. She hadn't meant to get so physical. But she had to make herself clear. No way did she want Becker showing up at the party and hovering at Faith's elbow all afternoon. "It's sort of a reunion of Faith's *old* friends," she said, trying to put it politely.

His face darkened. "I understand," he snapped. "I hadn't actually planned to show up."

He tried to shut the door, but Lauren pushed harder against with her shoulder. "Will you please give her my message?" she pressed.

Becker gazed contemptuously at her down his

aquiline nose, as if she were some kind of repulsive bug who had crawled onto his dinner plate. Even though she knew he was bad news, the look still made her feel like her old blobby self. How did he manage to do it? This guy was way too good at psyching people out.

"Of course I will, Laura."

That did it. "Lauren," she corrected, recognizing the oldest power play in the book. "You might as well know that I've done a little research on *your* friends, too. Like Jessica Danio, who just happens to be in my writing lab. That is, unless she gets kicked out of school for the letter you forged for her."

He jerked the door open. Lauren wasn't prepared for the sudden release of the weight against her shoulder and she stumbled forward and fell. He leaned down, grabbed her arm, and yanked her to her feet. The expression on his handsome face was blank and his voice was as smooth as silk, but the grip on her arm was savage. "So you came by here to tell that to Faith . . ."

"I just came by to tell Faith about a party," she interrupted, wrenching her arm out of his grasp and backing away. "Will you give her the message?"

"Yes," he said curtly. Then he slammed the door shut in her face.

Lauren swiveled away and stomped angrily down the hall toward the stairs, her blood boiling. What a creep! She was sorry she'd lost her cool, but she'd accomplished what she came to do. He'd probably give Faith the message. Still, it might not be a bad idea to make a point of sitting next to Faith in Western civ. and make sure that the message had been delivered. She'd make sure Winnie and KC came, too. That way they could be double and triple certain.

Where Becker Cain was concerned, nothing was too much.

"Did somebody come by?" Faith asked when she walked into her room only moments later. She'd seen a glimpse of blonde hair and khaki clothes hurrying down the stairs when she'd come out of the bathroom. It had looked like Lauren.

Becker immediately gathered her in his arms and ran his hands down the long curve of her back. He pulled back one corner of her collar and kissed the hollow of her neck. "Nobody important."

Faith opened her mouth to ask again, but before she could say anything else, his lips closed over hers. A hot fog settled around her brain and she felt her curiosity disappear for the moment. "Sorry I was gone so long," she giggled. "I ran into Kimberly Dayton. She wanted me to talk to her while she conditioned her hair."

"I don't mind," he said.

Faith looked up at his face. It was wearing that carefully neutral look he got whenever he was upset about something and it made her curious again. "It was Lauren, wasn't it?"

"You're right. It was Lauren." She felt his hands move to her waist and circle under her lacy blouse.

"Why didn't you tell her to wait?" Faith asked. Now that she had made the point that her room was no longer available as a drop-in crisis-intervention center, she would have enjoyed a little chat, just to hear what everybody was up to. She'd wanted to see them in Western civ., but had arrived too late to get her choice of a seat. She was beginning to miss her old friends.

Becker stared at her. "Lauren didn't give me a chance to ask her to wait. She just launched into some incoherent speech about having a personal problem and needing to talk to you about it."

"A personal problem! At ten o'clock at night?" Faith groaned, quickly revising her desire to chat with Lauren. "Not again."

Becker gazed sympathetically at Faith. His hands ran lightly up and down her back. "How do you stand it? She's supposed to be your friend. But Faith, a real friend wouldn't treat you like that."

Faith softened as his fingers pressed and caressed her narrow waist. She tightened her arms around him and relaxed against his chest. But she couldn't help wondering about Lauren. If Lauren had been willing to brave Faith's anger in order to seek her out at this hour, something must really be bothering her. "Maybe I should call her," she murmured into the neck of Becker's shirt. "If she really does have a problem I should . . ."

"Put her out of your mind for now," he whispered. He began to stroke her head, raking his fingers softly through her hair. "You've got to learn that not everyone who asks for your help really needs it," he purred. "People find their own answers to their problems if you let them."

Faith let her head fall forward, stretching the tense muscles in the back of her neck as his hands moved up and down her spine. Becker was right. Lauren would work it out.

"It's time someone helped you." His voice dropped lower and deepened.

His fingertips moved to the base of her skull, massaging it in a gentle, circular motion. "You can rely on me, Faith. You can always rely on me."

Faith began to feel dreamy and relaxed.

"Everything I do, I do for you," he said in a hypnotic monotone. "I am the only one who truly believes in you. I am the only one who truly wants to help you. I am the only friend you need."

Her eyelids fluttered heavily. She'd never felt so content. So at peace. Drowsy, and only half awake.

"We'll spend Saturday together," he continued in a lilting tone. "The whole day. We'll start with a picnic breakfast in the park. I'll make my special coffee. Then we'll go to the Laurence Olivier Film Festival. They're showing *Henry V.*"

Faith sighed.

"You'll enjoy that."

Becker's voice seemed to be coming from some-place far away. Faith was drifting now, barely hearing his words as they floated toward her. Faith gave up trying to follow what he was saying, and focused instead on the seductive rise and fall of his voice as his fingers continued their work.

Her eyes closed and her shoulders slumped as Becker's voice droned on, seeming to repeat the same phrase, over and over. ". . . Saturday together . . . Saturday together . . . Saturday together . . . "

*SATURDAY!*

Faith jerked her head up with a start and her eyes flew open. "Saturday!" she said out loud. "I *knew* there was something bothering me. Melissa's track meet is on Saturday."

"Faith!"

"I have to be there! She'll expect me to be there. I think I'm practically the only person she still trusts. I mean, I've barely seen her lately, but she's been so busy training. I don't think anybody's seen much of her."

"I heard the tickets are sold out," Becker argued.

"I'll talk to Melissa. She can probably . . ."

Abruptly, Becker removed his hands and pushed her away. "Fine," he snapped. He began to walk stiffly toward the door.

"What?" she questioned.

He stopped but did not turn around.

"Don't be angry," she begged, reaching out and catching at his sleeve. He turned and looked stonily at her.

"I'm not angry."

"Then don't be hurt."

His face grew pale. "Why shouldn't I be hurt? I love you. I've devoted myself completely to your interests. I've helped you study. I've organized your paperwork. Researched your theatre project. Got you into the finest university theatre program in the country. The only thing I ask for in return is one Saturday out of your life, and you tell me you'd rather go to a track meet."

"Becker."

"Of course I'm hurt!" he shouted. "What do you expect?"

Faith let go of his sleeve and fell back in stunned surprise. She'd never heard Becker even raise his voice, and now here he was shouting at her that she owed him something. From next door, Kimberly Dayton banged on the wall.

Faith ignored Kimberly's banging and stared at Becker's accusing face. It was strange and a little frightening. She didn't like seeing Becker act like this—so possessive and clingy. It made him seem small, mean, and very petty.

She took another step back. It was her own fault, she thought guiltily. She'd let things go too far too fast. Let him do too much for her. "I'm grateful for your help," she said in a shaky whisper. "But I think maybe we're spending a little too much time together, and I'm starting to feel a little crowded."

He didn't answer for a moment. Then his angry eyes softened and moved toward her. The next thing she knew, his arms were back around her and he was pressing his body against hers. "I'm sorry," he whispered in her ear. "I'm sorry. I'm sorry. I'm sorry." He laughed. "I'm acting like one of your *friends* now."

His lips moved up and down her neck and she let her head fall back with a sigh. It would be so much easier to think if he didn't have his hands all over her all the time.

"I just couldn't help myself," he breathed passionately. "I love you and you're the most important thing in my life."

Faith closed her eyes and forgot about Lauren, about Melissa's meet, and everything else as the fog closed in.

# Eight

"*L*et's get out of here."

Brooks stared stolidly at the "Men's Support Group" sign that hung on the empty podium at the front of the room. "It's okay if you want to leave. But I'm staying for the meeting."

Dash retied the red bandanna on his head and tugged at the neck of his dark green T-shirt. They were in a meeting room on the second floor of the Student Union. The room had no air or windows and it was depressing him. He didn't like the metal folding chairs. He didn't like the fluorescent lights. He didn't like the perforated acoustic tiles on the ceiling. He didn't like the orange industrial carpet.

And he sure didn't like the looks of the handful of guys who were sitting quietly waiting for the meeting to start. "Come on, Baldwin!" he whispered. "It's a waste of time."

Brooks folded his arms across the chest of his green striped cotton soccer shirt. "We don't know that yet. Give it a chance."

Dash blew out his breath impatiently. Brooks Baldwin was an all-right guy. Intelligent. Once in a while he was even funny. But he had that kind of lumbering jock determination that drove Dash crazy. He moved slowly and carefully. He talked slowly and carefully. And, Dash suspected, he thought slowly and carefully, too. Dash wondered if he should just split, quickly and recklessly. But he hated to leave Baldwin here by himself.

Dash had regretted signing up for this thing almost immediately. He'd had a feeling it was going to turn out to be something like this. He had meant to call Baldwin and cancel, but Tuesday had been so busy. Three classes. Two editorial meetings for the school paper. A couple of interviews with potential Olympic athletes. After that—an all-night writing session. Another editorial meeting this morning. A quick sandwich on the run. Before he knew it, it was Wednesday afternoon and Baldwin had shown up at the newspaper office to hustle him off to this shindig.

Dash glanced at the guy sitting to his right and shook his head in disbelief. Sheesh! Unbelievable! Little guy sitting there with no shirt, a few sparse chest hairs, and a tom tom made out of a coffee can. What are you *thinking*, pal?

On the other side of Brooks, there was a guy working on a needlepoint pillow with a watermelon motif. Dash shook his head again. If the guy was that desperate to keep his hands busy, why couldn't he whittle or something?

A fairly decent-looking redheaded guy stepped up to the podium. "Thank you for joining us," he said. "My name is Mitch, and I'd like to welcome you all to the first meeting of the University of Springfield Men's Support Group."

Dash began to feel slightly better, but then the guy with no shirt grunted and whacked the top of his coffee can—THUMP!—and the two guys sitting in the front row turned and stared for a moment. Dash's face turned red. This whole thing was just much too embarrassing for words.

"Thanks for sharing," Mitch said seriously.

Dash shot a look at Brooks to get his reaction. But Brooks merely settled his arms more comfortably across his broad chest and waited patiently for Mitch to continue.

Mitch looked out again across the room. "I

thought a good way to start might be to go around the room and have each person introduce yourself and tell us why you're here. Why don't we begin with the front row?"

There were two guys in the front row. One was tall and skinny, with blond hair. The other was big and beefy, wearing dirty gym clothes. They looked uncertainly at each other for a moment, neither of them wanting to go first.

Finally, the tall skinny guy stood. "My name is Jack. And I'm here because I feel alienated in what I perceive to be an increasingly feminized cultural and intellectual climate."

Several heads nodded seriously.

"Thanks for sharing," Mitch said. Then he gestured toward the other guy. "And you?"

The beefy guy stood up and his face flushed a deep red. "My name is Chuck. And I'm here because—get this. Last night, after three hours in the gym and a couple of laps around the track, I go over to my girlfriend's room to study. I come in. I get myself a soda. I settle down to hit the books. And you know what she says to me?" His voice rose in indignation. "She says to me, 'Chuck, you smell bad.'" Chuck looked around the room. "You believe that?"

Mitch frowned. "And how did that make you feel?"

"How did it make me feel? How did it make me

feel?" he repeated in a wounded voice. "I'll tell you how it made me feel. It made me feel . . . *smelly*!" And with that, he flung himself sulkily back into his chair.

Dash rubbed a hand over his face. This guy didn't need a men's support group. He needed a shower.

"Thanks for sharing," Mitch said. He jutted his chin in the direction of the second row.

The needlepoint guy calmly folded his work and stood. "My name is Joe. And I'm here to develop my feminine, nurturing side."

The room full of heads nodded again. *Get a grip, Ramirez!* Dash told himself, forcing his head to stop bobbing up and down.

Mitch pointed to the tom-tom guy. "My name is Kumbata," he said. He pounded the coffee-can tom-tom with gusto. "It is a cave name that I have given myself—to remind myself that I am a man!" THUMP! THUMP! THUMP! THUMP!

"I am here to discover my ancient, manly nature." THUMP! THUMP! THUMP! THUMP! THUMP!

Dash choked on a laugh, beginning to feel glad he had come. He hadn't written a humor piece in a long time. Maybe he was going to get a column out of this, after all.

It was Brooks's turn next and Dash wondered what Brooks could possibly find to say to these guys. "My name is Brooks." His voice was quiet and sincere. "I'm here because I'm confused about what a man is supposed to be."

In spite of himself, Dash was touched. For a lumbering jock, he'd put his finger right on it. That was the problem, wasn't it? They were all confused about what a man was supposed to be these days. Dash was horrified when he realized that there was a lump in his throat and a tear in his eye. He fiercely wiped his eyes. *That was the trouble with these kinds of things,* he thought angrily. They got people way too emotional.

"Thanks for shar—" Mitch began.

"Could we cut to the chase?" Dash interrupted. Enough was enough. The thanks-for-sharing jazz was making him queasy. He didn't want to hear it again. Besides, if they kept it up, he was afraid he was really going to start bawling.

"Cut to the what?"

"Cut to the chase," Dash repeated. He stood up. "The topic of this meeting is *What do women want?* That's what we're here to talk about. Let's get down to business." There. Now he had 'em on the ropes. If these guys had anything useful to say, let them go ahead and spill it so he could get back to the newspaper.

"Okay," Mitch said. "Let's move right to the topic." He pulled a piece of paper from his pocket.

"For purposes of discussion, I thought it might be interesting to solicit the female perspective. So I consulted one of the columnists from the school paper. You may be familiar with her work already, since she writes the 'HERS' column."

Dash felt his stomach clench. That column was really the 'HIS and HERS' column, with Lauren writing the female viewpoint and Dash writing the male.

"Ms. Turnbell-Smythe was kind enough to give me a copy of one of her upcoming columns. I'd like to share with you her thoughts on the subject." Mitch cleared his throat, unfolded the piece of paper, and began to read.

> "What do women want? Men ask this question all the time. Why? Why do men always assume that women want something? Maybe it's because men want something. The world teaches women to give, but it teaches men to negotiate. When a woman receives flowers, cards, and even apologies from a man, she knows he wants something in return. What do women want? They want men to quit negotiating and start giving."

Mitch folded the piece of paper and returned it to his pocket. "Now, do you have any comments?" he asked Dash.

Dash sat in his seat, so furious he could hardly

breathe. He could feel a vein in his temple throbbing and his stomach was tied up in six different kinds of knots. He looked around the room and every eye was looking eagerly at him.

"Negotiating!" he snorted, smacking his hand down on his thigh. "When a guy busts his butt to make things right with a girl, is that negotiating? When a guy send sends her flowers, is that negotiating? When a guy writes her letters, is that negotiating?"

"Not consciously. But maybe unconsciously," Joe suggested, threading his needle with green yarn.

"Right," Chuck said, jumping right in. His round, red face was flushed with enthusiasm. "What's the guy trying to do? What does the guy want?"

"What does the guy *want*?" Dash repeated. "Isn't it obvious? He wants to get back together with her."

"Exactly," Mitch said, smoothing his red hair down on his head. "It's obvious. Obvious that he's negotiating for something he wants."

"But what I . . . *he*," Dash corrected quickly, "wanted, was her. Does wanting her back make him a bad guy?" Dash waved his arms in the air. "All right!" he shouted in frustration. "So maybe he's negotiating. What else is a guy supposed to do?"

"Maybe doing something nice without tying a string to it would be nice," Jack suggested, turning in his seat to face Dash. "And do it in a way that doesn't make her feel pressured."

"Listen . . ." Dash sat angrily forward and lifted his finger, getting ready to deliver a speech about how women were impossible to please. But before any more words came out of his mouth, a light bulb went on in his head. *These guys are right!* he thought with a shock. As much as he hated to admit it, they were on to something. Dash closed his mouth with snap and sat back in his seat. He'd never really thought about just trying to do something nice for Lauren. He'd fought with her, competed with her, romanced her, chased her. But he'd never tried doing something nice for her just for the sake of being nice. Maybe it was worth a shot. He looked around at everyone's faces again and realized they were still waiting for him to say something. "Thanks for sharing," he muttered, feeling his ears turn pink.

Brooks sat forward and stared down at the knees of his jeans. He put his hands together and cracked his knuckles thoughtfully as the truth began to dawn on him. No wonder he'd blown it, first with Faith and then with Melissa. In both relationships, he'd thought he was being supportive, attentive, nurturing, and protective. But what he'd really been doing was a

Becker number. Negotiating for their love by fostering dependence.

Faith had broken up with him as soon as they'd arrived at school together. She was determined to stand on her own. Melissa had been such a loner at first. Brooks had spent months encouraging her to lean on him. Then, when she'd finally leaned, he'd walked away. No wonder she'd fallen on her face when he bailed.

Brooks looked around the meeting room. Mitch, Chuck, Joe, Jack, and the little cave guy with the coffee can were all busily talking to one another, but Brooks was too busy with his own thoughts to join in.

Brooks noticed that Dash looked pretty lost in his own thoughts, too. Dash sure was excitable sometimes. He looked pretty calm now, though. Maybe he was trying to figure out something nice to do for Lauren.

In his mind, Brooks was already turning over one or two ideas about Melissa. It was time he quit ducking into broom closets every time he saw her coming. It was time he quit cringing every time he heard her name. It was time he quit doing dumb things like setting up shrink appointments for her, as if he were some superior big brother who wasn't part of the problem at all.

She was a person, with real feelings and reactions.

The type of girl that somebody *should* do something nice for. Maybe he should give her a present to wish her luck on Saturday. He had a quilt in his room. A new one. His aunt had made it and sent it to them as a wedding present. It was still in the box. Giving Melissa a quilt would be a pretty nice thing to do, wouldn't it?

For a long time, Brooks thought about how happy Melissa would be to get the quilt. It would be a good first step. Who knew? Maybe they could even start being friends again.

He felt a hand yanking at his sleeve and then saw Dash's fingers waving in front of his eyes. "Yoo hoo, Baldwin. You in there?"

Brooks focused his eyes. "Sorry," he said. The meeting was over and the guys were standing up and filing out. He stood up and headed for the door, trailing behind Dash.

Most of the guys fell into step beside Dash, who by now was on friendly terms with the group. Brooks followed behind, listening to their animated conversation as they passed the various meeting rooms and offices that were located on the second floor of the student union. One door in particular caught Brooks's eye. It was the recruiting office for ROTC, the Reserve Officer Training Corp. Brooks stopped to get a better look at the poster on the door. It showed a young man in uniform, standing tall, straight, and confident with an eagle flying behind him.

Lots of students joined the ROTC to help pay for college. Or else because it guaranteed them an officer's rank if they opted for a career in the military. He knew about it because some of the recruiters had visited his high school.

*"The nice thing about the military,"* he remembered hearing the recruiter say, *"is that the rules are clear. There's one standard of behavior and it applies to everyone. Every man knows exactly what is expected of him, and what he expects of himself."*

Brooks continued to stare at the poster. That guy didn't look confused about what a man was supposed to be. Just like the recruiter had said, he looked as if he knew exactly what was expected of him and what he expected of himself.

"You coming, Baldwin?" he heard Dash shout. Brooks hurried to catch up with the group when he saw them going down the steps that led to the first floor.

"A real man isn't afraid to speak his mind," Dash was saying as he descended the steps.

"A man should know how to listen, though," Mitch said.

"I think a man should be vulnerable," Joe said as the group reached the first floor.

"But being capable and strong is important, too," Chuck insisted. He pushed open the heavy double-glass front doors of the Student Union.

Brooks stood outside on the front steps and only half listened as Dash and the rest of the group continued their discussion. He was busy trying to figure out how to wrap the quilt for Melissa. He still had the silver wrapping paper that had been around it when it arrived, but silver paper was for weddings. He should probably use a different kind of paper. Maybe he should use pink paper. Or was that sexist? Maybe he shouldn't wrap it at all. No. That was a terrible idea. A present should be wrapped. First thing tomorrow morning, he'd take the box over to the gift shop and ask them to help him pick some kind of suitable wrapping. He sighed unhappily. How did something so simple get so confusing all of a sudden?

# Nine

"You didn't get the food, or the plates, or anything?" Josh asked Winnie in stunned disbelief.

He pushed the pile of newspapers and Winnie's dirty breakfast dishes aside and dumped his knapsack and jacket on the kitchen table. Josh had just gotten home after an all night session in the computer lab and now he was looking unhappily around the disorganized kitchen. "Winnie! Today is Thursday and it's almost eleven. The party's forty-eight hours from right now. When I left for the lab last night, you said you were going to shop so we could start cooking today. I've got to do another all-nighter tonight. So if you want me to help you, we've got to . . ."

"I got something better than food and paper plates," Winnie interrupted. She grabbed Josh's hand and pulled him through the messy dining alcove and into the living room. "Look," she said, pointing proudly toward the hobby horse that sat in the middle of the messy living room. "I was on my way to the grocery store last night when I saw this in the window of the thrift shop. I couldn't resist."

Winnie giggled, remembering how the lady who owned the shop had been so interested in hearing about her baby. She'd made Winnie a cup of tea, let her sit in all the rockers, and told her stories about her own children. The grocery store had been closed by the time Winnie got there with the hobby horse tucked under her arm.

"Winnie," Josh said slowly. "This is great, but . . ."

Winnie knew what Josh was about to say. "Oh, I know there's tons of stuff we need more than this," she said quickly. "But Mom will probably get us all the practical stuff like the crib and stroller."

Josh rubbed his eyes and Winnie noticed the dark shadows beneath them. Poor Josh. Sometimes he was such a worrier. "Let's get back to the party for a second," he said.

Winnie took his exhausted face in both hands and

kissed him on the lips. "Relax. Mom's coming today. She'll help."

Josh looked unconvinced. "Sure, she'll help. But she's probably got things she needs to do while she's here and . . ."

Winnie shut him up with another kiss. "What could be more important to Mom than me?" she asked. She closed her eyes and hugged Josh happily. Once her mom found out she was pregnant, she probably wouldn't let her lift a finger for the party. "We'll probably sit up all night tonight talking about the baby, and tomorrow, we'll get ready for the party together."

"But, Win . . ."

Josh's thought was interrupted by the front door-bell ringing.

"She's here!" Winnie shrieked, practically knocking Josh over as she ran for the door, dodging the messy piles that covered the floor.

"MOM!" she shouted, flinging the door open. To Winnie's surprise, there were two people standing in the doorway instead of one. One of them was her mother, and one of them was a man. Winnie's mouth fell open in confusion. Her mom hadn't said anything about bringing a man along. Who was he?

Francine Gottlieb breezed through the door and kissed Winnie lightly on the cheek. "Hi, honey." She smiled over Winnie's shoulder at Josh. "Hi, Josh dear!"

Winnie stared at her mother. Her dark hair was still short and curly. And her figure looked great in her colorful gypsy skirt and red cotton top. Large chunky bracelets and rings covered her wrists and fingers. Her mom looked like her mom always did, but something was different.

"How are you, Francine?" Josh asked.

Winnie's mother sighed happily. "Absolutely wonderful." She turned toward the man who was still standing in the doorway. "Come in, Craig. Meet my daughter, Winnie, and her husband, Josh Gaffey."

Craig stepped into the front hall and Winnie's mom put a possessive hand on his sleeve. "Winnie. Josh. This is Craig Mather." Winnie noticed that her mother never took her eyes off Craig as she continued speaking. "Craig is a general practitioner. We work in the same building."

Winnie realized what was different. Her mother's eyes were sparkling like a teenager's.

Josh stepped forward and extended his hand. "How do you do, sir."

Craig shook Josh's hand. "Good to meet you, Josh."

"Are your bags in the car?" Josh asked. "I'll bring them in."

"No, no," Winnie's mom laughed. "Don't do that. We're not staying tonight."

"Not staying!" Winnie cried. This was terrible. "But I . . ."

"We just wanted to drop by and say hello. We're actually on our way to that new spa in Butte Falls. Craig is working on a book called *Healthy Vacations.*" She patted Craig's sleeve and then smoothed it. "He's a wonderful writer."

Winnie gaped. She couldn't believe her mother was actually gushing over this guy. He seemed okay enough, but he was nothing special. Medium height, sandy gray hair, semi-dumpy body, and glasses.

"We'll be back tomorrow," Dr. Gottleib said. "Probably around noon."

Winnie felt better immediately. "Great, Mom, because I'm . . ."

But her mom was already starting back out the door. She blew Winnie a kiss and took Craig's hand. "We've got to get going." She blew another kiss to Josh. "See you tomorrow."

Before Winnie knew it, her mother and Craig were gone. She ran to the window and watched them get into Craig's car.

"Looks like Francine's got a boyfriend," Josh said.

"Don't be dumb," Winnie grumbled. "It's just some weird phase or something. Probably empty-nest syndrome." Her mom would get over it when she knew Winnie needed her.

She felt Josh squeeze the back of her neck. "Come on," he said, kissing her ear. "Get your purse. Let's go shop before I fall asleep on my feet. Something tells me Francine's got better things to do than help us with a party."

Winnie pulled away from Josh and pressed her nose against the window, watching the car pull away. "I need to go take a nap," she said, suddenly irritated. Hadn't he been listening? "My mom will be back tomorrow and she'll help me then."

"Winnie!"

She turned and kissed him quickly on the cheek. "I need a nap," she insisted. She didn't want to get ready for the party with Josh. She wanted to get ready for the party with her mother.

"Okay," he agreed. "But will you at least start cleaning up later this afternoon?"

Winnie nodded. But she knew she wouldn't have time to clean that afternoon. She had Western civ. She'd promised Lauren she'd be at class early so they could save seats and talk to Faith. The party preparations could wait until tomorrow—when her mom got back.

The stands of the stadium were nearly half filled. *Not bad for a practice,* Melissa thought.

FRESHMAN OBSESSION • 103

Coach Terry settled his billed cap firmly on his head as he faced the runners assembled on the field. "Listen up," he shouted. "The big test is just two days away. Are we psyched?"

The runners all began to cheer and whistle. Melissa felt her grin reach from ear to ear. She caught a wink from Caitlin and they both happily pumped their fists and hooted. They were both getting unbelievable results from the stuff they were using.

Ever since Monday, Melissa had been exercising nonstop, and it was paying off big. During yesterday's run, she'd shaved another half second off her time. And the weight room had become almost an obsession. She'd skipped a lot of classes this week so she could work out. But she'd had another reason for going. She wanted to see the blond guy again. So far, though, he hadn't appeared.

"Everybody warm up and let's get started," Terry shouted.

Melissa squinted up into the stands at the crowd. Far in the back, she thought she saw a glimpse of golden-blond hair. "Caitlin," she said, bending over and stretching the muscles in her back. "Do you know anything about the blond guy in the wheelchair? The one who works out in the gym?"

"You mean the Incredible Hunk? Also known as the Mysterious Hunk," Caitlin joked.

"I guess," Melissa nodded.

"I don't know much." Caitlin bent her leg behind her and pulled on her toe to stretch the quad. "I just know that his name is Danny something and he lives in the dorms. I think his brother goes here, too. That's all I know."

"Do you know why he's in a wheelchair?" Melissa straightened up and shook out her arms.

Caitlin switched feet. "I think he had an injury. The chair is permanent. He's a good lifter, isn't he?" She grinned. "Why do you want to know?"

Melissa blushed and looked away. "Just curious, that's all. I met him at the gym. I just thought I saw him in the stands. No big deal." She didn't want to talk about what had really gone on in the gym on Monday night. It seemed much too intimate to share. She glanced up toward the stands again. There was no mistaking that blond hair. It had to be him. Was he here because of her? She couldn't seem to get him off of her mind, and it made her pulse race to think that she might be on his mind, too.

"There sure are lots of people in the stands," Caitlin grinned. "It's like the whole school is psyched. I've never seen so many people here to watch a practice run."

Caitlin was right. He was probably here for the same reason everybody else was—he was just interested in watching the runners get ready for the Olympic trials. Melissa felt a little flicker of disappointment. Then she shook herself. This was stupid. On Saturday, her whole life was going to change. She would be headed to the Olympics and she wasn't going to have time for a guy. Especially a guy in a . . .

TWEEET!

Melissa tensed at the sound of Terry's whistle.

"Runners for the 800, line up," he shouted.

Caitlin slapped Melissa on the back. "Go get 'em."

Melissa refused to look up into the stands as she jogged over to the starting line and took her place. She focused her mind on the race, refusing to think about his blond hair, his beautiful skin, his green eyes.

"What are you waiting for, McDormand?" Terry's booming voice brought her back to the present. With a shock, Melissa realized that the race had started and she was still standing at the starting line. She'd never even heard the starting whistle.

Suddenly filled with anger, she lunged forward to catch up with the pack. It took most of what she had to close the distance, but she managed to catch up as they took the first curve. What was wrong with her? She strained. She gulped air. She forced her mind to focus on her arms, her legs, her breathing. Everything was working now and the second straightway was a piece of cake. She took the curve again and pulled out ahead of the pack as they started the second lap.

Melissa thundered down the track, but as she hit the curve again, she realized she was paying the price for coming out too late and too fast. She was breathing hard and her legs were tightening up.

"Come on," she raged. *"Come on!"*

By the time she hit the second straightway again, she could feel the pack closing in on her. She poured on the speed, having to use every last bit of kick to keep her lead. The stopwatch in her head was running now. Her feet began to pound. If she could shave another half second today, she could . . .

"OUCH!" Melissa's face contorted and she gritted her teeth as a sudden stab of pain pierced her right Achilles tendon. It felt like somebody had suddenly clamped her tendon with a pair of hot tongs. The pain was excruciating, but she kept running.

She heard a roar from the crowd and wanted to curse them all. She was pretty sure she knew what that roar meant. A flash of purple and gold to her right confirmed it.

One runner flew past her, and then six more passed her by. Melissa slowed her speed with indignation and rage.

Terry shook his head in disbelief as she thumped over the finish line. "Next time you fall asleep at the starting line," he shouted, "I'm going to wake you up with the back of my hand."

Melissa glared at him.

The coach began to laugh. "We're lucky this was only practice. Get out of here. You've been working too hard. Get some rest."

Terry strode off to confer with one of the assistant coaches and Melissa trembled with humiliation. What a stupid thing to have happen, but it was lucky, too. This way he wasn't asking a lot of questions, like . . .

"Are you limping?" she heard Caitlin's voice gasp as she veered off the track.

"NO! Yes. I don't know," Melissa snapped. "Just don't say anything to me for a minute, okay?" Melissa's body was bathed in a cold sweat and she began walking in circles, trying to make the tendon stop hurting. It wasn't easing the way it usually did after a flare-up. This couldn't be happening. Not now. Not two days before the Olympic trials. She squeezed her hands until the nails dug into her palms.

"Mel, what is it?" Caitlin begged.

"What am I going to do?" Melissa whimpered in panic. "It's the tendon again. It really hurts this time."

"'Roid dungeon," Caitlin said. "I've got some painkillers. I'll meet you there after my run. It'll get you through Saturday. After that, you can rest for a few weeks." Caitlin put her hand on Melissa's shoulder. "You'll be okay."

"NO! It won't be okay!" Melissa exploded.

Caitlin stepped back. "Hey, don't go 'roid raging on me," she whispered.

Melissa swallowed and forced herself to breathe deeply. "I'm sorry," she said, reaching out to put her hand on top of Caitlin's. Her hand trembled.

"Hey, no problem. What are friends for?"

Caitlin jogged away to join the other sprinters, and Melissa picked her gear up off the ground thinking how quickly things could change. Not long ago, she'd hated Caitlin and loved Brooks. Now, she hated Brooks, and the only person she really trusted was Caitlin.

The tendon hurt as she walked away from the field, but she made herself put her weight on it so the limp wouldn't show. There was a little pricking feeling as the hair on her arms stood up. She wondered if it was the pain or if it meant a pair of green eyes were watching her from the stands.

# Ten

.................

"**W**ill you give this to Melissa?" Brooks asked as soon as Lauren opened the door of her room. He awkwardly thrust a large, beautifully wrapped gold box into her arms. "It's for good luck."

"Do you want to come in and wait for her?" Lauren asked. "She had a practice run this afternoon, but she should be back soon."

"No," he answered quickly.

Lauren caught the note of alarm in his voice. Brooks Baldwin was the most fearless soccer player on campus. But he had been a major coward when it came to facing Melissa.

"I've got class in a couple of minutes and I'm probably going to be late as it is," he explained. "Besides, I'll see her at the party, right?"

"I don't know," Lauren said. "I've hardly seen her since last Monday. She's out of here at the crack of dawn and I'm usually asleep by the time she gets back from the gym. I thought I'd talk to her about the party when she got back from practice."

Brooks nodded and Lauren thought he looked pale. "Okay. I told Dash about the party, but I'm not sure he's coming, either." He put his hands down into his pockets and coughed nervously. "I'll see you Saturday," he said.

Lauren watched him back out the door. Then he hurried down the hall like it was all he could do not to break into a run.

She stepped back inside the room and shut the door. Then she took the box and carefully put it on Melissa's bed.

Actually, she didn't blame Brooks. Melissa had been incredibly moody lately. Sometimes she was on top of the world and really friendly. Sometimes she was surly and impossible to get along with.

Lauren didn't have very long to think about it, though, because within a few minutes, the door opened and Melissa burst in.

"Hi, there," Lauren said, trying to make her voice

sound cheerful. "Practice went well, I hope. Didn't it?"

Melissa grimaced but didn't answer. She clutched at her foot, then collapsed on her bed. "What's that?" she asked, pointing to the present on the bed.

"Brooks brought it by for you."

"Brooks?"

Lauren nodded. "And Winnie is having a party on Saturday. It starts at noon and it would be great if you came and . . ."

"The Olympic trials are on Saturday," Melissa snapped. "You know that."

Lauren flinched. "I know," she said softly. "But the party starts at noon, and I thought you might be able to come by for a few minutes. It's really a party for Faith. We're sort of hoping that everyone will come and we can all mend our fences."

"Does that mean Brooks is going to be there?"

"Yes."

"Then don't count on me." Melissa reached for some scissors and snipped the ribbon off the box. She tore the paper away and lifted the top.

Lauren peered over her shoulder. "How beautiful!" she breathed.

Inside the box was one of the most beautiful quilts Lauren had ever seen. There was a note folded neatly on top. Melissa opened it with a snap and began reading aloud in a flat, angry voice.

*Dear Melissa,*

*This quilt was sent to us as a wedding present from my aunt. She told me to keep it and not send it back. I thought that it might be something you would like to have. Maybe it will help you remember some of the good things about our relationship and forget the bad. Good luck on Saturday.*

*Brooks*

"That's really sweet," Lauren said. In spite of the fact that Lauren thought Brooks had treated Melissa pretty badly, she had to admire him for trying to make amends.

"SWEET?" Melissa screamed.

The ferocity of her response startled Lauren and she jumped back, staring at her roommate with fear.

"You think it's sweet?" she yelled. Her body began to shake with an uncontrollable anger. She was already a wreck from what happened at practice. She didn't need this.

Melissa tried to control herself. It was the drugs, she reminded herself. She knew it was the drugs. It had never happened to her before, but she'd seen it in the lifters and even with Caitlin. She tried to breathe deep, but she couldn't stop what was happening. Rage was surging through her body like a tidal wave. Caitlin had given her some pain pills and injected her with another round of steroids for good measure. She wasn't in pain anymore, but she did feel totally out of control.

Melissa grabbed a pair of scissors lying on the desk and in one swift movement, she slashed the quilt from one end to the other.

*"Melissa!"* Lauren leaped forward. She grabbed at the quilt, but Melissa jerked the box away and began ripping at the delicate fabric with her hands.

"Why would I want something to remind me of the most humiliating day of my life!" Melissa spat.

"Stop it," Lauren begged. "I know how you feel. And I don't blame you. But please don't . . ."

Melissa's upper lip lifted in a snarl as she tore wildly at the quilt. "How can he think I'd want anything from him. Or his family. Or from anybody who's ever known him—including you!"

Melissa saw Lauren lurch toward the door, mumbling something about her two o'clock Western civ. class and Melissa needing time alone. But Melissa wasn't listening to Lauren anymore. She was too busy feeling the quilt coming apart in her hands. She tore and ripped and shredded until her arms ached with the effort. Then she fell across her bed, suddenly exhausted.

Coach Terry was right. Melissa needed rest. She'd been running or lifting almost nonstop since last

Monday. First thing tomorrow morning, though, she
would show Brooks what she thought about his present. She would go to his dorm, and finally, once and
for all, let him know exactly what she thought—
about *everything*.

# Eleven

........................................

**F**aith hurried into her Western civilization
class a few minutes before two and took a
seat at the back of the large lecture audi-
torium. Sue, the teacher's assistant, was returning
exam papers to the students who were there.

Sue smiled at Faith as she fished her exam out of
the stack in her arms. "You sitting alone again?"

"Looks like it," Faith smiled, taking the exam. She
flipped it open, smiled at the *A* penciled on the top,
and then shoved it into her book bag.

"How come you don't sit with your friends anymore?"
Sue asked. "I used to think of you all as the middle-row
gang. Now you're up here by yourself all the time."

*I'm up here because I had to keep some distance from them,* Faith thought. But at the same time, she was looking around the lecture hall, hoping to see the middle-row gang. Actually, she was starting to miss sitting with Winnie, KC, and Lauren.

"What's the topic for the next research paper?" Faith asked quickly changing the subject.

"Queen Elizabeth I." Sue smiled. "She was quite a woman. Ought to be right up your alley."

Faith laughed.

Sue moved on down the aisle.

"Hi!" said a familiar voice. It was KC, looking around as if she were supposed to meet someone.

"What are you doing here?" Faith asked, surprised as KC plopped down in the seat next to her.

"Here in this class? Or here in this lonely back row?" KC tossed back. She sat down and opened her briefcase.

Faith laughed. "Never mind. How are you?"

KC smiled. "Great."

Faith hadn't seen much of KC recently. KC had missed a lot of classes during her father's illness, and was still working overtime to make up the work. And of course, she was always busy with the Tri Beta sorority. Faith was glad to see KC looking almost like her old self. "You look good," Faith smiled.

"Thanks," KC responded. "Things are going great at the sorority house, and Cody and I are getting closer every day. He takes the hard edge off my life, I guess. And it's more than that. He's a pretty special guy."

Faith began to relax. It was a lot easier to talk to KC now that she was back on an even keel. Faith didn't feel like she had to go chasing after KC to keep her out of trouble, and since KC never called her anymore, Faith interpreted that to mean that KC didn't want to be taken care of.

Becker was right. Too many of Faith's friendships had been about dependency and caretaking. *You spend all your time worrying about your so-called friends,* he had said once. *When was the last time any of your friends demonstrated any real interest in what was going on in your life?*

"How are things going with you?" KC asked, as if she were reading Faith's mind. "I mean, how are things *really* going? How's work in the theater department?"

Faith smiled slowly. "I got into the Professional Theater Program. So I'll be able to work on extra productions and take special classes my sophomore year."

"That's fabulous!" KC said and gave Faith a quick hug. "How did you get in? You told me once that almost no freshmen make it."

Faith shrugged. "I came up with a concept for a new production of *The Taming of the Shrew*. Well, actually, Becker helped come up with the general concept, and I worked out all the details. But if it hadn't been for Becker, the whole thing never would have happened. You can't believe how helpful he is and what a difference he's made in my life."

KC's face fell a little. "Faith, don't you think he's a little *too* helpful?"

Faith sat up straighter. She suddenly wished that Dr. Hermann would arrive and start his lecture. "What do you mean, *too* helpful?"

"Faith, he follows you around night and day," KC said. "It's like he wants to take over your whole life. I've tried to call you, but you never called me back. Becker took the messages. I finally decided that he never told you I called."

Faith felt her face begin to flush. Actually, she had been there once when KC had called. But she hadn't been in the mood to listen to anybody else's problems, so she'd asked Becker to tell KC she was out. Later, she'd forgotten to return the call.

"He did give me the message," Faith said, not wanting KC to think badly of Becker. "And I forgot to call you back. I guess I've been busy. I'm sorry."

"You forgot to call me back five times?" KC asked. "That's pretty forgetful."

"You called me *five* times?"

KC nodded. "Three times at your dorm. And a couple more at Becker's dorm."

So KC was right. Becker *hadn't* given her the messages. Becker's white and angry face floated up in front of her and she felt angry, too. What was he trying to do? Make sure she never made up with her friends? She remembered the tirade she had treated him to during the Co-ed by Bed experiment. She'd been going crazy trying to work on her *Taming of the Shrew* proposal. After about the fifth interruption from her friends, she had just flipped out and spent two hours complaining about all her selfish friends. He had taken her ravings seriously. So how could she be angry at him? He was just trying to help, she told herself. He just wanted to make an environment in which she was free to create and not get bogged down in other people's problems.

But before she could say another word, Winnie came in wearing purple tights, a Hawaiian shirt, and fringed white ankle boots. "Yo," she grinned.

Lauren rushed in a half a second later and Faith sighed as the girls forced her to move down two seats to make room for all four of them.

"Is something going on?" Faith finally asked, beginning to suspect a conspiracy.

Winnie grinned. "It's old-home week. Shall we sing Auld Lang Syne?"

"How are you?" Faith smiled.

"Totally scattered as usual, and totally freaked," Winnie laughed. "Mom's got some guy—but I don't think it's serious. At least I hope it's not."

"Really?" Faith exclaimed.

"Have you met him?" Lauren laughed.

Winnie nodded.

"What does he look like?" KC demanded.

Winnie made a face. "His name is Craig Mather. He's a doctor. He looks like . . . you know, your average, nice, normal doctor. Anyway, you can see what he looks like on Saturday, because he and Mom will both be at our party."

"You're having a party?" Faith asked.

Winnie's face froze. She threw a look at KC, who shrugged, and a look at Lauren, whose eyes narrowed.

"Our reunion party," Lauren said slowly. "Didn't Becker tell you? I came by your room Monday night to tell you, but he said you weren't there. He promised to give you the message."

"You came by to tell me about a party? But Becker said that . . ." Faith blushed and her voice trailed off. Becker had told her that Lauren had wanted to talk about a personal problem. Becker had actually . . . *lied* to her. It was one thing not to pass on phone messages, but to actually lie to her was a deliberate act of sabotage. She sighed heavily. Becker was getting out of hand.

Lauren, Winnie, and KC were all looking at her. Faith nervously wet her lips, trying to think of something to say.

Fortunately, she didn't have to say anything, because

Professor Hermann stepped up to the lectern and rapped on it. "Let's get started," he announced.

"Take notes for me, will you?" Faith whispered to KC, pulling her book bag into her lap and zipping it.

"Aren't you staying for class?" KC exclaimed.

Faith shook her head. "No," she whispered in a shaking voice. "There's something I have to do."

"What about the party?"

"I don't know."

"Faith!"

"Look," Faith whispered. "We've got a research paper coming up for this class. Elizabeth I. Let's meet tomorrow at the library and work together. We can catch up then. Around three o'clock. Okay?"

"Faith!"

But Faith was already stumbling over Winnie's and Lauren's feet and hurrying toward the door. The drone of Professor Hermann's voice got fainter and fainter as she ran down the hall past the Junior Year Abroad posters and the "OLYMPIC FEVER" streamers that were tacked on the walls.

Outside, her cowboy boots made an angry clopping noise along the concrete walkway. *Stay angry. Stay angry,* she told herself. *If you don't stay angry, you'll never make him understand how you feel. If you don't stay angry you'll be in his arms and wind up in the fog wondering what it was you meant to say.*

The angry clop clop changed to a determined thump thump as she veered off the walkway and cut across the grass. Her feet were coming down so hard, the heels of her boots left little half moons in the grass.

"Hi, Faith!" a voice shouted as she passed the Theater Arts Building. Faith lifted her hand and waved it in the air, but she didn't turn to see who it was. She kept her eyes focused on the flat roof of Becker's dorm.

She galloped up the front steps two at a time. Her boots echoed loudly in the empty hallway as she approached Becker's door, shoved the key in the lock, and pushed the door open.

Becker sat at his desk, bent over a textbook. He was wearing a pair of jeans and no shirt. His hair hung down on either side of his face. He didn't even look up when Faith entered the room. Becker was capable of incredible levels of concentration. Against the stark white walls of the room, his still, naked upper torso looked like a statue in a museum.

Faith closed the door firmly behind her.

Becker's head jerked up and then his startled face took on a pleased, surprised look. "Faith! What are you doing here?"

"Why didn't you tell me about the party?" Faith demanded.

"Party?"

"The party Lauren told you about." Her voice was

firm, but she couldn't keep the little quaver out of it.

Becker stood up slowly. He pushed his dark hair back off of his high brow and began moving toward her. She tried not to look at his broad shoulders and smooth chest.

"Becker," she said, stepping back as he lifted his arms and reached toward her. "Why didn't you tell me about the party?"

His arms dropped to his sides and he shrugged. "Because I didn't think you should go," he answered casually.

"Shouldn't that be my decision?" she cried.

Becker caught Faith's hand and brought the palm to his lips. "I'm glad you came over," he breathed into her hand. "I've been working all day and it's time to stop thinking about myself and just think about you again. You're so talented, Faith. But you don't know how to protect your time or your talent. I do."

"You should have given me the message!" Faith protested, snatching her hand away. "I told you why I broke up with Brooks my first week here. He thought he was supposed to protect me, too. You don't help me by being just as protective. Creative ideas don't happen in a vacuum. They come from life. From people. If you cut me off from people, you cut me off from my creativity."

She turned toward the door, put her hand on the knob, and jerked the door open. "You have to let me make my own decisions. Is that clear?"

Becker's hand shot out over her shoulder and pushed the door shut. She flinched as he spun her around to face him.

Faith stood trembling with her back pressed against the door. Becker leaned down until his face was an inch away from hers. Her heart began to pound. Was it attraction or fear that was making her heart beat so fast?

"I hesitate to remind you, Faith, that the best idea you've had all year came from *me*!" Becker said. His voice was low and intense with controlled anger. "If it hadn't been for *me*, you wouldn't have had a concept for your proposal. If it hadn't been for *me*, you wouldn't have gotten into the Professional Theater Program. If it hadn't been for *me*, you'd still be avoiding your own life every time the phone rang." He stopped and took a deep breath. "I love you, Faith. Doesn't that give me any rights at all?"

His face moved closer and he leaned in to kiss her. But she put her hands against his chest and pushed him back as hard as she could.

"NO!" she shouted. "It doesn't. I didn't ask you to fall in love with me. I didn't ask you to help me with my theater project. I'm grateful for your help. But those were your decisions. It doesn't give you the right to run my life."

Shock and amazement were written all over his face. His brows knitted in bewilderment. "What am I to you?" he demanded in weary frustration. "I've given everything to you. Aren't you willing to give me anything in return?"

"I don't know right now," she answered. It was the truth. Right now she felt hemmed in, pressured, and too angry to sort through her jumbled feelings.

Becker's lips tightened as he looked at her for a long, long moment. Then he seemed to make a decision. He leaned forward and pushed her aside gently so that he could open the door. He stood in the open doorway with one hand on the knob, and the other on his hip. "I think you'd better make a decision. Make it by Saturday. If you love me, you'll skip the party and spend the day with me. We'll go to the film festival."

"Becker!"

"If you don't love me . . ." He stared down at the floor. "I need to get on with my life. I'll drop by your room on Saturday between twelve and one to see what you want to do." His hand left his hip and guided her firmly out the door.

Faith couldn't believe what was happening. Was he really going to turn this into an all or nothing situation? Couldn't they even discuss it? "Becker," she began.

But his face was set in hard lines. Faith caught a last glimpse of the question-mark poster on the wall just before the door shut quietly in her face.

Faith walked slowly down the hall, her book bag

thumping against her hip. She didn't like ultimatums. She was beginning to dislike things about Becker. But she did still like Becker's attention and his help, and she was still definitely attracted to him. Was she at all ready to let him go?

"Hey! Turnbell-Smythe!" Dash was leaning against the red brick wall that surrounded the Literary Arts Building. He was wearing his red bandanna and a two-day stubble.

Lauren's heart dropped when she saw him. The last thing she needed right now was a confrontation with Dash. It was six o'clock and she was always exhausted by the end of her Thursday afternoon writing lab. And she felt especially tired today because of the fiasco in western civ. She, Winnie, and KC still didn't have an answer from Faith about Saturday. Now they just had to hope KC could talk some sense into her tomorrow at the library.

Dash walked toward her and Lauren thought his face looked more friendly than she remembered. It also looked sexy, annoying, and funny, but Lauren tried not to think about that. What did he want, anyway? Maybe he was just going to tell her he was looking forward to the party. Still, she kept the expression on her face as distant as possible. Even the most innocuous conversations with Dash somehow turned into battles of wits or wills. She didn't want to get drawn into one now.

"You're not going to make this easy, are you?" he commented. Dash scratched his head and then pulled the bandanna down a bit. "I'm trying to do something nice for you, and you're staring me down like you think I'm about to mug you."

"Why do you want to do something nice for me?" she asked in a flat tone, hoping her lack of interest would inspire him to keep this short.

He shook his head. "You're hopeless."

She removed her wire-rimmed glasses, polished them on her shirt, and then put them back on. If this conversation was about the party, he sure was taking the long way around to get to the point.

"I got a little peek at your next column," he admitted. "They read it out loud at the Men's Support Group meeting."

"You went to the Men's Support Group meeting?" Lauren asked. She started to smile, then tried not to giggle. Dash was usually so cynical. It didn't seem like something he would do.

"Yeah. Me and Baldwin."

Lauren smothered a laugh, remembering the last line of her column. *Women want men to quit negotiating and start giving.* She had meant it figuratively. Boy! Guys sure were literal sometimes. Now she understood the motivation behind Brooks's present to Melissa.

Poor Brooks. He had completely misunderstood.

She wondered what Dash was going to come up with, and she couldn't help chuckling out loud.

"Okay, okay," he said quickly. "No laughing, please. This is hard enough without you guffawing in my face." He pulled an envelope from his hip pocket and held it out to her. "Here. This is for you."

She hesitated.

He rubbed his face. "It's not a letter bomb. It's not hate mail. It's a gift. From me. There's no string attached to it. This is not a negotiation."

She took the envelope. "What is it?"

He gazed back at the buildings. "It's an application for an internship at West Coast Woman magazine. I saw it advertised in a writer's bulletin. They take one Springfield student each year for a two-week assignment. The winning student gets to help write an article and hopefully have it published. I thought you might like to know about it."

"And it's open just to women?"

"No."

"But you won't be applying?"

"Nope. I'm not challenging you to a competition. Not this time."

"Do you think I *can't* compete with you?"

He rolled his eyes. "Would you please just read the information?"

Lauren opened the envelope and began to read. West Coast Women magazine was a national magazine whose offices were in downtown Springfield. They wanted recommendations and an essay, and Lauren could tell it was right up her alley. It was thoughtful of Dash to tell her about it. Really thoughtful.

"Thanks," she whispered. Then she lifted her eyes to study Dash's face, waiting for some kind of line. He'd given her something. Now he would want something in return. Probably an apology for having been all wrong about him.

But Dash just smiled. "You're welcome. So I'll see you around."

Lauren jerked her head in surprise. Was he really just going to do something nice and then leave it at that? Maybe he was. "Okay," she said.

He backed away, but continued to watch her face. "I'm going now."

" 'Bye."

"I'm not going to ask you out, or anything like that."

"All right."

He shoved his hands in his pockets and turned to walk away.

For the first time in weeks, Lauren was sorry to see him go. "Dash!"

He turned.

"Are you going to be at Winnie's party Saturday?"

"I might be if *you* invite me," he admitted.

"You're invited," she said.

"Do you want me to be there?"

"Dash."

"Yeah?"

"Don't push your luck."

# Twelve

**M**elissa tried to shift the cardboard box under her arm, and as she did, shirts, pictures, programs, dried flowers, and the remains of the quilt fell out on the dewy grass. All the mementoes of her relationship with Brooks Baldwin were stuffed into her cardboard box. Every memory. Every souvenir.

"Darn!"

Melissa dropped the box angrily and began to scoop the things up. It was still early and the air was cool. But Melissa was sweating from exertion and anger. She couldn't wait to walk into Brooks's room and dump the whole box over his head. She couldn't wait to tell him what she thought of him and his stupid quilt. Couldn't wait to call him a dirty, cowardly, jilting, *weenie.*

From her kneeling position, she could see a variety of athletic shoes stepping over her and her junk as the residents of Rapids Hall, the outdoor-pursuits dorm, hurried to their early-morning activities. She stood up and hoisted the box again. A pair rugby jocks stood talking outside the front door and she shoved past them, ignoring their surprised faces.

Once inside, she didn't wait for the elevator. She couldn't wait. The morning round of 'roids were pumping through her system and she had to keep moving.

Melissa opened the fire door and took the stairs two at a time. Angry tears began to roll down her cheeks as the whole awful scene kept replaying itself in her head. . . .

*"Do you, Brooks, take Melissa, to be your lawful wedded wife?"*

*Brooks just stood there in stricken silence.*

*"Brooks," the minister prompted.*

*Brooks. Hanging his head. "I'm sorry. I can't do this."*

Why? Why couldn't he do it? He had pursued her so relentlessly. He had begged her to marry him, overridden her objections. He'd broken through her defenses by saying that he loved her. And she'd believed him. Her throat and chest felt so tight, she could hardly breathe. Just thinking about it made her heart ache with unbearable pain and anger.

She heard the stairwell echo as she kicked the door open and stomped onto Brooks's floor.

Melissa pounded on his door with the flat of her hand.

No answer.

She banged again.

Nothing.

Melissa balled her hand and banged on the door with her fist until the heavy wooden door rattled on its hinges. More and more, her anger filled her whole body, made her feel like she could rip the world to shreds.

Why did he stop loving her? What had she ever done to him? What had she done wrong? Nothing. Nothing except hand him her heart to break.

"I hate you Brooks Baldwin!" she shrieked, not caring who heard. "And I'll hate you until the day I die!"

She threw the box against the door with all her might and watched the cardboard split open. The contents scattered along the floor. Melissa stepped back, breathing heavily, still not satisfied. Her blood was still pumping. What she wanted was a face-to-face confrontation.

She wiped the tears away with her sleeve and walked slowly away from the door. Her Achilles tendon was bothering her, so she decided to take the elevator down. Great. She was going to need more painkillers. She'd better find Caitlin before she went to the morning practice run. Her shoulders felt tired and heavy. Suddenly she realized that she needed some kind of release. She had to tell off somebody before her race the next day—and that somebody had to be Brooks.

By the time the doors opened again on the first floor, Melissa had made a decision. Lauren had said Brooks would be at Winnie's party tomorrow. She would go before the meet and let him know once and for all how she felt.

"And I can't wait," she moaned as she stepped outside again.

The morning air was still cool and Melissa began feel a little calmer. To take her mind off of her tendon, she rehearsed the scathing things she would say to Brooks. Halfway across the dorm green, she felt the hair on her arms stand up. She looked around. She had that somebody-is-watching-me feeling again.

*I'm getting paranoid,* she thought, quickly looking around.

That notion scared her. She knew that paranoia came along with steroid use, just like the uncontrolled rage.

Then she suddenly stopped. Someone *was* watching her. Across the dorm green, she saw a familiar pair of green eyes and a head of shimmering blond hair. He lifted a gloved hand and gave her a tentative wave.

Automatically, Melissa's hand rose and fluttered.

He began to wheel his chair in her direction.

Melissa felt like kicking herself. Why had she waved? She didn't want to talk to him. Not after what had happened at practice. She was sure that he'd seen her, looking like a total loser. She didn't even know him, and he was already messing up her head. Besides, if he was so interested, why hadn't he shown up at the gym again?

But he seemed eager to speak with her. As his chair got closer, his smile grew broader.

"Hello!" he said. "At last, we meet again."

"Hi," Melissa nodded curtly. He was wearing bulky grey sweatpants again and a tight white T-shirt with short sleeves. When he extended his hand to shake, she noticed the muscles straining against the fabric of the shirt.

"We were never formally introduced," he said. "I'm Daniel Markham. My friends call me Danny."

Melissa managed a tense smile.

"Is that the best you can do?" he asked.

"What do you mean?"

"I mean I've seen happier faces in coffins. What's the matter? That right leg bothering you again? It looked like it was bothering you after your practice yesterday."

Melissa bristled. What was he trying to start here? "You're wrong," she bluffed. "My leg is fine."

His mouth fell open in surprise at her antagonistic response, then he made a quick recovery. "Oh, yeah," he said sarcastically. "Mine, too. There's not a whole lot I can do for mine, though. What are you doing for yours?"

"I'm resting it," she admitted grudgingly. "Not that it's any of your business. And not that there's anything wrong with it."

He chuckled and shrugged. "If that's your story, stick to it. I'm not your coach. But if I were your coach, I'd be concerned about that leg—along with a couple of other things."

"What other things?"

He lifted one golden eyebrow. "Let me put it this way. If I were a coach and I saw one of my star runners spending a lot of time with the bodybuilders, I'd take that runner aside and have a very serious heart to heart."

"What are you implying?" she asked angrily.

He smiled again. "I'm not *implying* anything. I'll spell it out for you if you want. Let's just say that I have friends in the weightroom. Guys talk."

Melissa stopped breathing.

"About what?"

Danny squinted, studying her face. "Is it my imagination? Or are your eyes beginning to look a little yellow?"

Melissa's face began to grow pale. She knew exactly what he meant. He was talking about steroids. Enough use caused liver damage and made the whites of users' eyes turn yellow. But that hadn't happened to her yet. Had it? She tried to laugh.

"Is it funny?" he asked.

Well, let him speculate. He didn't know anything for a fact. Couldn't prove anything. And he wasn't her coach. "Well, if you hang out with bodybuilders, then you know it's no big deal," she said, deciding that the best defense was a good offense. "Besides, I've seen you in the gym. You like to stay in shape."

He looked right at her. "Sure. I work the weights. But I stay natural. And to answer your question, I've got nothing against bodybuilders. But some of those guys are fooling themselves in a very dangerous way. Steroids are just another form of substance abuse."

She turned on her heel and began to walk away. People in wheelchairs were supposed to be sensitive and vulnerable, not know-it-all jerks.

"Hey!" she heard him shout behind her.

Melissa kept walking.

"Hold it!"

She turned.

"I just want to know one thing."

Melissa waited.

"What the hell have you got to be so angry about?" He wheeled the chair quickly over to where she stood and looked up at her with serious green eyes. "I mean it. What's got you so pissed off?"

"You wouldn't understand," Melissa snapped.

He let out a long sigh. "Wouldn't understand what?

Wouldn't understand the pressures of competition? Wouldn't understand the desire for perfection? Wouldn't understand feeling that your whole life rides on the results of a race? Believe me. I understand."

She finally looked at him. "How?" she dared to ask.

"I was a big jock, too," he admitted. Then a wave of sadness covered his face.

"Track?"

"Baseball."

"So you weren't always in a . . ." she broke off in embarrassment.

" . . . always in a wheelchair?" Danny finished for her. "No. I wasn't born with a chair stuck under my behind."

Melissa felt even more embarrassed and she didn't know which way to look. Maybe it wasn't something he wanted to talk about. Maybe it was something *she* didn't want to talk about. She just knew that it was time to get out of this conversation before she said something stupid.

"Look. I don't really have time to talk right now, but . . ."

"Fine. Then *I'll* talk," Danny said with great purpose. "I have to talk to someone. So I'll tell you about the wheelchair. I know you're curious."

"No I'm . . ."

"Sure you are," he insisted with a little anger of his own.

Melissa didn't move.

"You know, people think it's rude to be curious, or even interested. So they pretend they don't see me. Believe me, I'd rather deal with the curiosity than be invisible."

Melissa managed a nod.

He met her eye for the briefest second. "So anyway. Where was I? Oh yeah. It was a dark and stormy night, senior year. Daniel Markham had just hit two home runs in the final game of the season. The baseball scholarship was in the bag and Daniel Markham decided to celebrate. He didn't use drugs. Drugs were for junkies. Daniel Markham didn't need drugs to feel powerful and invincible. He felt powerful and invincible already. So powerful and invincible that after the game he thought he could gulp down a half-fifth of vodka with his teammates, then get into his vintage Volkswagon Beetle and drive it into a tree going sixty miles an hour. And you know what?"

Melissa couldn't speak.

He adjusted one of his fingerless leather gloves. "It turned out that I wasn't the iron man after all. Nobody is that powerful. Nobody is that invincible. I severed my spinal cord, spent a year in a hospital and rehabilitation center, and wound up sitting here in a wheelchair trying to tell a pretty girl that substance abuse is substance abuse is substance abuse."

"I see," Melissa whispered.

He lifted his eyebrows and dropped his voice in a ironic aside. "And you thought this story wouldn't have a moral."

Melissa was stunned. She was on the verge of tears. But a moment later she was also so mad, she thought the top of her head just might blow off and go clattering along the sidewalk like a hubcap. How dare he lecture her? Who did he think he was?

"Leave me alone!" Melissa shouted.

"No," he said pleasantly. "I don't think I will."

Melissa felt the explosive rage building inside her again. It was time to bring out the big gun. The double-barrel McDormand special. The most effective pest control in the world. She twisted the features of her face into an ugly frown—and turned it on him full force.

But all he did was stare up at her face with a fascinated expression. "Wow! I bet most people find that look very intimidating."

Melissa tried to hold the expression, but it was impossible. "What?" she managed.

He reached out and poked her stomach, then whistled. "Hard as a rock. Or is it just that everything inside her has turned to stone?"

Melissa looked down at herself. She still wanted to be angry. She tried to stay angry. But for some reason this time it faded a little. She was so aware that Danny was still smiling at her. He hadn't been intimidated by her rage. It was nice to be able to yell at somebody and not have them completely fall apart. Brooks hadn't been able to handle anger at all.

Danny just kept smiling. His hands shifted a drawing pad in his lap.

"What's that?" she asked, noticing the thick tablet for the first time. "Are you an artist?"

"I draw," he answered, picking up the pad and beginning to flip through it. "It's no substitute for stealing bases, but it keeps me out of the pool halls. Wanna see?"

She nodded.

He opened the drawing pad and held up a page.

She was stunned. And . . . pleased. It was a picture of her. A sensitive pen-and-ink drawing of her face and shoulders. The drawing was beautiful.

"When did you do that?" she asked, feeling incredibly flattered.

"A few days ago. Mostly I do cartoon-type illustrations, though." He flipped through the tablet until he found a second sketch. He tore it off the pad and gave it to her. "Keep it," he said.

Melissa looked down at the drawing and gasped. It was a cartoon drawing of her running a race. But she didn't look beautiful in this picture at all. In fact, she looked hideous. He'd drawn her as a huge belly with great big bulging muscles. In the cartoon her foot was stuck out at an angle, directly in the path of another runner.

Anger billowed in her chest again like a hot air balloon. "I've never tripped another runner in my life!" she shouted.

He swiveled around and stuffed the pad into a backpack that hung on the back handles of the wheelchair. "No? Well, you're cheating, just the same. And eventually, cheaters get caught." The upper part of his body turned back toward her and he smiled blandly up at her.

Melissa tore the drawing in half. Then she tore the halves into little pieces and threw them at him.

"How dare you?" she bellowed.

"Want to go out to dinner tonight?" he asked as the tiny pieces showered over him like confetti.

"NO!"

"I didn't think so." He threw back his head and began to laugh. The blond hair shimmered and glowed under the sunlight as he brushed the confetti away with his gloved fingers.

Melissa glared for a moment. Then she turned on her heel and ran away. She couldn't believe she had wasted five minutes thinking about Daniel Markham. He was a self-righteous, sanctimonious, insulting *jerk*!

# Thirteen

"There's tons of stuff on Elizabeth I in here."

KC dropped an armload of books and periodicals on the long wooden library table and sat down next to Faith. "And for once, the research material looks interesting."

"Elizabethan England was an interesting period," Faith said. She removed one of the pencils that were stuck into her braid and began to flip through the pile.

KC took off her blazer and draped it over the back of the old-fashioned wooden chair. She picked up a heavy theater book full of glossy photos and waved it playfully in front of Faith. "I brought this especially for you. It's a book on contemporary interpretations of Elizabethan drama."

Faith's fingers tugged nervously at the sleeve of the lace peasant blouse she was wearing over her jeans. It was Becker's favorite blouse, she thought idly. Hers, too. Their tastes were exactly alike in so many areas. Literature, theater, books, food, clothes. There weren't many guys she could say that about. She noticed that KC was still waving the book in front of her face and waiting for a response.

"Great," Faith said weakly. "It looks fascinating."

"You don't look fascinated," KC said. "And you don't look very happy, either. Want to talk about it?"

Faith sighed. "Becker and I had a big argument about his not telling me about the party."

"What did he say?"

"That he was trying to protect me."

"Protect you from whom? Protect you from your friends?"

Faith swallowed nervously. That was exactly what he had been trying to do. And in spite of what Faith had said to him, she wasn't convinced he was wrong. She did let her friends dump their problems in her lap. And they did drain an enormous amount of her energy. Energy that would be better spent on creative projects and schoolwork.

But she couldn't say any of that to KC. "He means well, KC," was all she said.

"Does he?" KC stared at her with a gleam in her eye, as if she were trying to make up her mind whether to tell Faith something.

"Yes," Faith insisted. "He does." There was no getting around it. Becker might be possessive, but he had done more for her than any other guy she had ever met. Who else would have stayed up all night with her helping her with a theater proposal?

"Whatever you say." KC chewed on her lower lip with the air of someone determined to say nothing. Then she began to flip through the library book. "Sometimes people with good intentions can do pretty serious harm," she finally muttered. "And a lot of people are going to be disappointed if you don't show up at the party tomorrow."

"Becker hasn't done me any harm," Faith snapped. "He's done me a lot of good. He's made me see a lot of things more clearly. And if it weren't for his idea to set *The Taming of the Shrew* in the old west, I wouldn't have gotten into the Professional Theater Program. Then all I'd have to think about right now would be Elizabeth I, and you and Lauren, and Winnie and Brooks, and all the rest of my so-called *friends* and their problems!"

Faith's lip was trembling and she felt tears welling

up in the corners of her eyes. She hadn't mean to say all that. What had gotten into her? How could she be so insensitive?

But KC didn't look hurt. And she didn't look angry. She was staring down at the theater book in her hands with a flabbergasted expression. "You're setting *The Taming of the Shrew* in the old west?" she asked in a soft whisper.

Faith swallowed and wiped her nose with a tissue. "Yeah. Petruchio is an outlaw. And Katherine wears six guns and. . . ."

"And this was *Becker's* idea?" KC interrupted.

"It was his concept. I did all the scene work and . . ."

"Oh, Faith!" KC wailed. She shoved the book toward Faith. "Look!"

Faith snatched the book from KC, and when she looked down at the two-page photo spread, her heart stopped. "Oh no!"

In front of her eyes were photographs from the Seattle Shakespeare Festival's 1977 production of *The Taming of the Shrew* set in the old west! Complete with a black-hatted Petruchio and a six-gun-toting Katherine.

"Oh no," Faith whispered. The contents of her stomach begin to churn as a horrible suspicion occurred to her. With trembling fingers, she turned to the back and removed the library's check-out. Her eyes ran down the names of the students who had checked the book out. Right at the bottom, she saw Becker Cain written in a neat hand.

"No!" Faith let out a little scream and dropped the book on the table. Her hands flew to her face but she couldn't even feel her skin. It was numb with shock and fear.

It was all clear now. Becker had gotten the idea from this book. Then he'd fed it to Faith and let her apply to the Professional Theater Program with it. He had used someone else's idea. That was called plagiarism. And people got expelled for plagiarism.

*I did it because I love you,* she remembered him saying. What kind of a person would do this to somebody they loved? She lowered her hands slowly, dragging the trembling fingers along her cheeks and raking them with her nails. "I'm dead," she shuddered.

KC was looking at the check-out card now. She shot a look at Faith and shifted uneasily in her seat. "You're not the first," she said darkly. "Becker did something like this to another girl."

"What do you mean?" Faith whispered hoarsely.

KC took a deep breath and cleared her throat. "I'm not supposed to tell you this, but . . ."

\* \* \*

Josh raced into the kitchen with another bag of groceries. He had gone back to the store three times since their big shopping trip that afternoon to get the last items they had forgotten.

"What time did Francine say she was going to be here?"

Winnie brought the big kitchen knife down across the carrot she was slicing with a loud *thwack!*

"Noon," she answered shortly.

It was almost seven and Winnie hadn't heard a word from her mom. She had waited for her all afternoon, sitting stubbornly in the living room until Josh had finally put his foot down and insisted that they get started, Francine or no Francine.

The two of them had rushed out and bought paper plates and groceries. But Winnie was so miserable and disappointed and angry at her mother that she couldn't enjoy the shopping or the cooking or anything else. It was obvious by now that her mother wasn't going to show.

"Maybe you should call and check on her."

Winnie brought the knife down again.

*Thwack!*

"Nope," she said. "If Mom would rather be in Butte Falls with that guy than here with me, I'm not going to chase after her."

Josh opened the broom closet, took out the

dustpan and broom, and began to sweep floor.

"Don't you think you're being a little oversensitive?"

"I'm pregnant. Being oversensitive comes with the territory. If you don't like it, you can split."

*Thwack!*

Josh lifted his hands in frustration. "Would you cut it out? I'm not going anywhere."

"Then I'll leave."

Josh went back to his sweeping. "Okay, fine. You leave. But do me a favor and wait until after the party. I'm not sure I can handle it on my own."

Winnie's lower lip protruded. How could he make jokes when he knew how unhappy she was?

"I was kidding!" he said, dropping the broom and hurrying over to the sink. He put his arms around her waist and kissed the back of her neck. "I love you." He kissed her again. "I need you." He kissed her again. "And you're making me very nervous with that knife."

Winnie dropped the knife in the sink and began to sob. "I want my mother," she wailed, bending over and letting her tears fall into the soapy water. Even though Josh was here, she felt completely abandoned. Completely overwhelmed. And wounded to the core. Nothing in her life had ever hurt her as much as her mother's indifference.

Josh gently turned her around to face him and hugged her. "I know."

"I want to tell her about the baby," she sobbed, throwing her arms around him and pressing her face against his shoulder. "I want her to be here for my party. I want her to fix some of her special stuffed mushrooms. I want her to talk to all my friends. I want her to make a big deal about the baby and act like she's happy about everything and . . ."

"I know. But Winnie, there could be a good reason why she's not here."

"Like what?"

"Like they had car trouble."

"She would have called."

"They could have been abducted by aliens."

Winnie didn't laugh.

Josh snapped his fingers. "That's it. Why didn't I think of it before?" He nodded, his face serious. "You read about it every day in the papers, but you never think it's going to happen to someone you know. The authorities really ought to do something about it."

Winnie finally managed a weak chuckle. "Let's write a letter to our congressman."

Josh drew himself up. "Write a letter! Are we people of action or not? I'm calling the president and I'm calling him now."

Winnie laughed into a dish towel as Josh marched toward the phone.

But just as he reached it, the phone rang. He picked it up. "Hello." He smiled in Winnie's direction. "Hello. Francine! Yes. She's right here."

Winnie's heart lifted and she raced to the phone. Josh was right. She was being oversensitive. Her mom and Craig were probably stranded somewhere with car trouble. Her mom would never just not show up and not call.

"Mom?"

In the background, Winnie could hear latin music playing and glasses clinking.

"Winnie?"

"Where are you? What happened? Are you okay?"

A silvery laugh floated through the phone. "Of course I'm all right. We're still in Butte Falls."

"Still in Butte Falls?" Winnie frowned. Maybe they had a fender bender in the parking lot at the spa and were waiting for their car to be repaired at the local garage. Or maybe Craig had gotten sick from all that healthy food and her mom couldn't leave him. Or maybe . . .

"We are having an absolutely fabulous time here. You can't believe this place."

That was not what Winnie wanted to hear. "Mom!" she said, trying to keep her voice from sounding as angry and hurt as she felt. "I was expecting you this afternoon."

"We drove up to a little place in the hills to have lunch and before we knew it, the day was gone so we decided to stay another night."

"Why didn't you call?"

"I meant to, but I forgot." Her mother laughed. "We'll be there late tomorrow afternoon."

"But the party starts at noon."

"Party?"

"I'm having a party tomorrow! I tried to tell you yesterday but you left so fast. I'm having a party for Faith. It starts at noon. I was expecting you to be here for it. In fact, I was expecting you to . . ."

"How nice. Tell Faith . . ." she heard her mother's voice break off into giggle. "Oh, Craig," Winnie heard her mother laugh.

"Mom!" She wanted to reach through the phone and shake her mother. Did she think Winnie wanted to listen to her mom flirt with some guy?

"I'm sorry, honey. I really am." Her mother was speaking directly into the phone again. "This sounds important to you. We'll be there in time for the party if we can."

Click.

After a moment, Winnie hung up, too.

She saw that Josh was watching her with a very nervous look on his face. He moved his hands from his hips to his pockets, and then back to his hips.

Then he reached for a dish towel and began to wring it between his hands. "Well?"

"My mother is totally immature, totally inconsiderate, and totally irresponsible!" Winnie exploded.

Josh held up his hands. "Now, Winnie, don't get . . ."

Winnie snatched the dish towel from his hand and slapped it against the counter. "Here I am, needing her more than ever. And instead of being here, she's doing the samba or something with Dr. Frankenstein."

"Mather."

"WHATEVER!"

Winnie jerked open the door to the refrigerator and resentfully surveyed the week-old cartons of juice and milk, and the suspicious-looking containers of leftovers. "None of the food is ready. The house is a mess. I'm pregnant. And she doesn't even care!"

She grabbed the handle of the industrial-sized garbage can, dragged it over to the refrigerator, and began to throw things out to make room for the party food.

"Winnie!" Josh said, dodging her as she moved around the kitchen. "She doesn't even know!"

"And whose fault is that?" Winnie yelled, hurling a bag of moldy bread into the garbage can. A sack of mushy onions followed. Then she burst into uncontrollable sobs. "How can I tell her anything if she won't listen to me for five minutes?" she choked.

Josh put his arms around her. "Please don't get so upset. It's just a party. We can get ready for a party without your mom."

Winnie sobbed harder. It wasn't just the party. It was everything. How was she ever going to cope with a child if she couldn't depend on her mother anymore? Who was going to take care of her while she was taking care of the baby?

Brooks picked up the little piece of paper and stared at it. It was an old ticket stub to a soccer game. A game that had been played weeks ago. He'd been at that game with Melissa.

"What is all this?"

He glanced down the corridor. There sure was a lot of litter along the hall. Brooks had been away from the dorm all day at classes and soccer practice. He'd found this mess waiting for him when he'd come back.

He stood, dropped the ticket stub in the hall wastebasket, and continued toward his room. A few steps later, something else caught his eye. He bent over to get a better look at it. It was a concert program. The program to a concert he and Melissa had gone to together.

He looked to his left and noticed a paperback

book. *The Art of Running*. He'd given a copy to Melissa.

Brook's heart began to beat uncomfortably and he started to run. Something was wrong. Something was way wrong.

Then he turned the corner that led to his room and came to a screeching stop.

Shirts. Papers. Ticket stubs. Dried flowers and . . .

Brooks bent down and retrieved a small piece of fluffy fabric. The edges of the fabric were torn and frayed, as if Melissa had ripped it apart with her hands.

He crumpled the piece of fabric in his hand and stared dumbly at the wreckage. *I blew it!* he thought in wild confusion. *I was trying to be nice, but I did the wrong thing. Again!*

He gritted his teeth. Large, hot tears began rolling down his cheeks and his shoulders began to shake. He'd never felt so horrible in his life.

"Oh, Melissa!" he choked. "I wish I knew how to stop hurting you!"

# Fourteen

"**W**ow! You are pumped!"

"To the max," Melissa confirmed, restlessly pacing the length of the 'roid dungeon. She looked at her watch. It was almost noon. Time for the final showdown.

"I can't believe this day has come," Caitlin said. "But we've got almost two hours before we're due on the field. Terry doesn't even want to see us warming up on the track too early. He thinks we'll just get freaked."

"I won't get freaked," Melissa said.

"What are we going to do to kill some time?" Caitlin put the syringes back in the gym bag. As she zipped her bag up, she added, "What I gave you will take care of the pain in your tendon. It's just a temporary thing, so after this race, you can finally rest your leg. But you shouldn't feel a thing today."

Melissa nodded. "Thanks."

"I hate this waiting around! Want to hang out in the weight room for a while?" Caitlin exhaled. "We could bug the guys up there. I just hate standing around getting nervous."

Melissa reached up, grabbed a low-hanging pipe, and chinned herself. She'd never felt so strong. So powerful. So aggressive. She felt like she could tear that pipe out of the wall and swing it back and forth like a bat. And bring it down on Brooks Baldwin's head.

"I'm not going to hang around here. I'm going to a party," Melissa said with tigerish smile.

"A party!" Caitlin repeated. "You're going to a party *today*? Before the pre-Olympic trials? Are you crazy? Go somewhere and meditate. Stretch. Or listen to the tapes that the sports psychologist made for us. You've got to hit that track like you're going to conquer the world. Step on it and grind it under your feet."

Melissa released her grasp on the pipe and dropped to the floor in a fighter's crouch. "I'll be psyched after this party. This is just the psychological warm-up I need. Don't you worry." Melissa snatched up her gym bag and was out the door before Caitlin could argue anymore.

Outside the Athletic Complex, the campus looked

like a carnival had come to town. TV trucks and camera-men were putting down long cables and unloading large cameras. Spectators were beginning to stream into the stadium, and student vendors were hawking University of Springfield pennants and T-shirts that said "GO FOR THE GOLD".

Melissa walked past the stadium, across University Avenue, and off campus. As Melissa marched down the tree-lined street of Greek Row, she noticed that several of the fraternity and sorority houses had streamers and posters tacked to their front doors in honor of the meet.

She walked faster, stood taller. The whole world was on her side. It was hard to believe that not long ago she'd been hiding under her bed covers like the world's biggest loser. Brooks had made her feel that way. Thinking about Brooks jump started her anger and dispelled the excited feelings that were welling up inside her.

A fraternity guy with long blond hair stepped out on the porch of the ODT house and whistled loudly. "Aren't you on our team?" he called out.

Melissa nodded.

"Go for the gold!" he yelled.

"I sure will."

The fraternity guy's blond hair reminded her that there was somebody else who *wasn't* on her side. Danny had made it pretty clear that he didn't approve of what she was doing. Thinking about the conversation with him made her feel even angrier. That was good. The anger was getting her more pumped with every step.

Melissa quickly left Greek Row behind. She passed apartment and rooming houses, and finally turned down a street crammed with rundown rental bungalows and a few old houses that were well kept up. By the time she knocked on Winnie's door, she felt like she could conquer the universe. The door opened and Melissa saw that Winnie was wearing pink tights, high-heeled purple boots, and a bathrobe.

"Melissa!" Winnie's face registered happy surprise. "I didn't expect you to be here, but I'm totally thrilled." She gave Melissa a hug and then took her hand and pulled her into the house. "Welcome to the most disorganized party in the world." Her fingers danced on the top of her head, nervously pulling up her spiky hair. "I guess you could say this party has a do-it-yourself theme."

Melissa looked around the living room and decided it looked like somebody had raked junk into neat piles in every corner.

"Don't be so hard on yourself, Win," Cody Wainwright was saying as he flipped through the CDs. "I like an all-hands-on-deck approach to party planning." He looked up and smiled at Melissa. "Hey! Glad you could make it. We're honored to have a real, live Olympic candidate here today."

Winnie stepped into the closet, closed the door, and then reappeared a few seconds later in one of Josh's t-shirts. "Josh and I worked until late trying to get stuff ready. We didn't get very far though, because I got upset and had an attack of morning sickness—at night. I guess I can't eat tacos and jelly beans at the same time anymore. So then we wound up oversleeping and didn't wake up until KC and Cody rang the bell. Then everybody started arriving and . . ." Winnie grinned at Melissa again. ". . . and why am I telling you all this when what I should be telling you is *good luck*! We are so proud of you."

Melissa just stared at her.

Josh came running out of the kitchen alcove with a tray of chips and dip and placed it on the dining-room table. KC was hard on his heels with a plate of cookies.

"Hi, Melissa," Josh said. "Good luck today."

"We're going to be watching you on TV," KC smiled. As usual, KC looked crisp and well turned out in a pair of black wool slacks and a white sweater. "We couldn't get tickets. It's been sold out for days."

Next Lauren and Dash ran through the room, each with an armload of dirty clothes. They looked like a couple of guerrilla dry-cleaners in their parachute pants and T-shirts.

"We couldn't find the laundry basket," Lauren was

telling Winnie. Where do you want us to put . . ."
She broke off and came to an abrupt halt when she
saw Melissa. Dash bumped into her and dropped the
load in his arms.

"Just shove it under the bed," Winnie instructed,
too rattled to notice the tension between Melissa and
Lauren. She rubbed the top of her hair. "We're supposed to be having a party to show Faith how much
we care about her, and this room says, *we don't care
very much.* But we'll get it together."

"Are we even sure that Faith is coming?" Lauren asked.

Melissa was starting to wish *she* hadn't come. The
place was a mess. Everybody was in a weird mood.
And Brooks was nowhere in sight. She shoved her
hands down into the pockets of her warm up jacket.
"Listen. I can't really stay. I just wanted to . . ."

But before she could finish, the swinging door that
led to the kitchen opened and Brooks appeared in
the dining alcove.

"Okay," he was saying. "I've iced down the sodas
and . . ." The rest of his sentence died on his lips
when he saw Melissa.

A sudden pump of adrenaline threatened to knock
Melissa off her feet and she let out a strange sound,
almost like a growl. *At last. Brooks Baldwin in the
flesh.* She froze, feeling like a tiger who was about to
stalk her prey.

Brooks froze. The two stared at each other for a long moment. Everybody in the room seemed to freeze, too. The air crackled with tension.

Then, suddenly, everybody seemed to begin talking at once. Cody turned on the music, and rock and roll began thumping in the background. KC, Lauren, and Winnie developed an urgent need to rearrange the dips on the table. There was a slightly hysterical quality to the sudden flurry of activity as it swirled around her, faster and faster, like a tornado. Melissa could even hear the wind of the twister as her body began to shake with anger.

She watched Brooks take a deep breath, then he slowly crossed the room.

"Can I talk to you?" he asked quietly. "About the quilt and the stuff you left in my hall?"

Her hands were shaking now. Her knees were jerking. She even felt her jaw ache as a tidal wave of rage came surging up from her feet.

Brooks shifted. "I wasn't trying to push your buttons," he explained. "I wasn't trying to be a jerk. I was trying to do something nice." His voice sounded strained and emotional.

That was when something bright and hot exploded behind Melissa's eyes. "Nice!" she yelled, as the tidal wave broke over her brain. "You thought you were doing something nice?"

Brooks paled and took a step back. Dash, Cody, and Josh suddenly appeared in the background behind Brooks. Melissa's eyes darted from face to wary face. They unconsciously moved closer together, standing shoulder to shoulder, like a line of defense behind Brooks.

KC, Winnie, and Lauren began moving in from the dining room to join them. *They're surrounding me*, Melissa decided. They were ganging up. Everyone was out to get her.

"Melissa," KC began. "We know . . ."

"Don't," Lauren said quickly. "Let her say what she wants to say. It's time we all listened."

Having Lauren defend her just made Melissa explode again. "Shut up, Lauren! This is between me and Brooks!"

Josh stepped forward and coughed nervously. "Melissa, if you and Brooks would like to go upstairs and talk, we can. . . ."

"I don't want to go upstairs," Melissa yelled. "I want to say what I have to say right here."

Brooks began to blush. "Whatever you have to say to me, I probably deserve," he said in an agonized tone. "But can't we talk in private?"

"No!" Melissa brought both hands down furiously on the back of a chair, knocking it over. She knew she was losing control. But she didn't care. It felt good. It was like falling out of an airplane, or destroying something for the thrill of it. Besides, she was powerless to stop herself.

"Did you think you were doing something nice when you made me fall in love with you? Did you think you were doing something nice when you asked me to marry you? Did you think you were doing something nice when you dumped me?" she shouted.

Winnie hurried toward Melissa. "Melissa. We're your friends. Why don't we all . . ."

"Don't touch me, Winnie," Melissa warned. She hadn't meant to scream so loudly, but now that she had started, she couldn't stop.

Winnie was coming closer.

"Don't touch me," Melissa growled.

Winnie's arms were closing around her.

"I said, don't touch me," Melissa pushed her away with a savage shove. "Leave me alone!"

Winnie tumbled to the floor with a cry and Josh dove forward to help her. "Winnie!"

Melissa stumbled back, appalled but exhilarated. That one little act of physical violence seemed to satisfy something inside her. And she wanted more. A strong hand closed over her upper arm.

"That's enough," Brooks said.

Something about the sight of Winnie on the floor, the frightened stares, and most of all, Brooks's cool assuming of authority sent Melissa spiraling over the edge.

"I hate you!" she shrieked, wrenching out of his grasp. Her body was shaking and it felt like her brain was shaking, too. There was no stopping this. This was more than pump. This was an overwhelming rage that had a grip on every ounce of her being.

"I hate you all!" She stumbled back several steps and snatched up a large glass bottle of mineral water. It felt heavy. She waved it and aimed at Brooks's head.

"No!" Winnie sobbed, holding up her hands.

"Don't, Melissa!" KC screamed.

All around her, Melissa saw mouths move and faces contort. But all she heard was the whooshing sound of the wind and the waves. She opened her eyes wider and her brain seemed to open up, too. Everything that was happening now started to feel like it was happening in slow motion.

Cody and Brooks lurched forward slowly, as if they were moving through glue.

Melissa's arm drew back. All her movements now felt slow, dancelike, deliberate, and completely unreal. She squinted at Brooks's head, taking aim. Her arm bent back and then flung forward. She felt the neck of the bottle slip out of her palm.

The bottle sailed through the air, turning around and around as it spiraled toward Brooks.

His curls snaked up as his head moved downward. It was like Melissa was watching it happen underwater.

As he ducked, the bottle missed his head by less than an inch. Melissa was mesmerized by the journey of the bottle shattered against the wall behind Brooks.

Crash! The splintering sound broke the slow motion of the scene and was followed by an ear-splitting scream from Winnie. Now everything was fast forward, a terrifying jumble.

"Nobody touch the broken glass!"

"Somebody grab her!"

"Winnie, are you all right?"

"Stop or I'll call the police!" a different angry voice suddenly shouted.

This voice was older, more authoritative. The sound of it brought Melissa up short.

She whirled and saw a middle-aged brunette woman with short curly hair standing in the doorway, dressed in jeans and a gypsy blouse.

"Stand still," the woman ordered, pointing a stern index finger that wore a chunky ring. Beside her, a tall man hovered protectively.

"Mom!" Winnie sobbed, lifting herself off the floor and stumbling toward the door.

The woman threw her arms around Winnie. "I don't know who you are," she said to Melissa. "But I want you to leave my daughter's home. Right now."

Melissa whipped her head around. There were people staring at her from every corner of the room. KC, her lip curling slightly. Cody, his face carefully blank. Winnie, looking tearful and childlike. Josh, torn between anger and sympathy.

And Brooks stood in the middle of the room, his eyes shut tightly as if he were in unbearable pain.

*Good!* Melissa thought grimly. *Good! I've finally managed to hurt and humiliate Brooks, the same way he hurt and humiliated me.*

Then she ran blindly for the door, pushing past Winnie and her mother and stumbling out the door.

Once on the street, she began to jog, gulping the air into her lungs. Soon she slowed to a walk. She moved more slowly, finally noticing that she was passing Greek Row again. The campus was in sight.

She saw the stadium and thought eagerly of the race. But at the same time, as her heartbeat began to slow, and the blood ceased its insistent throbbing, she began to feel flat, empty, and ashamed.

Winnie's hurt and bewildered face floated up in front of her and Melissa began to feel physically ill. What had she just done? God. She had pushed a pregnant woman to the floor. She had hurled a potentially lethal bottle at Brooks, actually wanting to hit him.

Melissa stopped at the street corner to catch her breath. On the faces of her friends, she had seen pity, fear, and anger, but most of all disgust, she realized. They had looked at her as if she were some kind of repulsive freak. Or a huge ugly bully with big bulging muscles.

She caught a glimpse of her reflection in a car window and froze. Her eyes. Something about her eyes looked different.

Melissa leaned closer to get a better look and gasped. They were turning yellow. No one else would notice it yet. But she saw it. She knew.

*That's it*, Melissa decided. *After this race, I'm through.* The steroids were taking their toll on her body and warping her personality, turning her into a real-life version of the horrible cartoon character in Danny Markham's drawing.

Melissa started back toward campus and winced at the stab of pain in her right Achilles tendon. It was hurting now with every step. She must have strained it during her 'roid rage. The painkiller she had taken this morning was wearing off. Or worse, it was taking more and more of the stuff to be effective.

Caitlin had given her some pain pills to keep in her room. Melissa knew what she had to do. She would swing by and take them before she went to the stadium. She would have to hurry, but she didn't have a choice anymore. She had come this far, and she couldn't turn back now.

# Fifteen

F aith sat on the end of her bed and stared at the door. She knew that Winnie's party had probably started. And she knew that her friends were waiting for her. But right now, it was more important to get things straightened out with Becker.

Faith had spent most of yesterday afternoon and evening in tears or in terror, trying to figure out what to do. It was only a matter of time before somebody else stumbled across that photo story on the Seattle Shakespeare Festival's production of *The Taming of the Shrew*. And when they did, Faith was going to be in horrible trouble.

She dropped her head into her hands. What had Becker been thinking about when he did this to her? Didn't he care about her at all? KC told her he had done practically the same thing to another girl. Now that girl was on academic probation for submitting a forged letter of recommendation. Plagiarism was ten times worse than that.

Faith sat back on her bed and studied the bulletin board that hung over her desk. It was a short history of all her freshman-year theater projects. There was the program from *Stop the World, I Want to Get Off.* Below that hung the program from the production of *Alice in Wonderland* that she had directed. Tacked in the corner were pictures of herself with Merideth, her best friend in the department, taken the night they had worked until three in the morning to straighten out a scenery problem for the student One-Act Festival. There were lyric sheets, rehearsal schedules, ticket stubs, an usher's pin, and a dozen other things that symbolized her hard work and dedication.

None of that was going to offset the crime she had unwittingly committed. A sob rose in her throat. Everything that she loved was represented on that bulletin board. And Becker had managed to turn it all into rubbish.

There was a sound at the door. She tried to compose her face as the lock clicked and the door swung open.

It was Becker.

He walked into the room and smiled. "I knew it. I knew you wouldn't let me down," he said. He wore baggy black pants, a white shirt, and his oversized sport coat—his usual movie-going outfit. Obviously, Becker was planning to go out, and he assumed that Faith was planning to go with him.

Faith didn't return his smile. "Becker," she said, working hard to keep her voice steady. "I don't want you to walk in without knocking anymore."

Becker moved swiftly toward the bed. Sitting down beside her, he brushed his long fingers over her face and neck. Faith twitched impatiently. His touch didn't excite her now. It felt too practiced. Too manipulative. And his fingers didn't feel cool anymore. They just felt cold and that made her shiver.

He pulled her head onto his shoulder and ran his hands up and down her arms. "You're unhappy and it's my fault. I'm sorry about Thursday. I didn't have any right to threaten you like that. Of course you should make your own decisions. Do whatever you want to about the party. I won't be angry."

Faith pulled away, rolled across the bed, and stood up on the other side. She reached into the pocket of her jeans and pulled out the key to his room.

"Here," she said, tossing the key on the bed. "Take your key and give me back mine."

"This key is a sign of trust. Mutual trust," Becker whispered, closing his hand around the key to her room. "Don't you trust me anymore?"

"How can I trust someone who let me apply to one of the most prestigious theater programs in the country with a *stolen* idea?"

Becker's eyes went flat. "You're mistaken," he said abruptly.

"There's no mistake, Becker. I saw the article about the Seattle Shakespeare Festival production. The same article you saw. And I know you saw it because your name was on the check-out card of the book. How could you do it?" she demanded.

He got up, came around the bed to where she stood, and circled her waist with his arms. "Whatever I did, I did for you," he said softly, his voice becoming low and caressing. "Because I love you. Because your ambitions and desires are my ambitions and desires. You wanted to get into the program. I helped you get in. It was a gift from me. Why is that so hard for you to accept?"

"Because I can't accept stolen goods," she said, exploding with anger and breaking out of his arms.

"I wish you would quit using the word *steal*. *Things* can be stolen. *Ideas* can be shared. Or borrowed. I don't believe in taking a proprietary attitude toward journeys of the mind."

"It doesn't matter what you believe. It's what the Professional Theater people will believe. And they're going to believe I'm a phony. A fake. A thief. I applied for that program with a stolen idea. It's called cheating, Becker. And if they catch you at it, you get expelled from school."

"You're not going to get kicked out of school," he laughed. "If you start exaggerating dangers, you'll start being afraid to take risks."

Faith swallowed. He didn't see it as a moral issue. He saw it as a matter of risk assessment. Okay. If that's how he wanted to debate it, she would do it his way. "You're right. I probably wouldn't get kicked out of school. But I would definitely get kicked out of the Professional Theater Program."

Becker shrugged. "That is a possibility. But so what?"

"So what?" Was he crazy? What did he mean *so what*?

He crossed his arms over his chest and leaned back against her desk and Faith thought she had never seen anybody look so totally arrogant in her whole life.

"So you get kicked out of the University of Springfield Professional Theater Program," he said. "I doubt it will happen. But so what if it did? There are other theater programs. There are other schools. There are all kinds of ways to get what you want, Faith. If necessary, I'll find the ways. I'll do whatever it takes to get you what you want."

"How dare you make a decision like that for me." she accused. "How dare you just casually decide to expose me to a risk like this without telling me. This isn't about me getting what *I* want," Faith said bitterly as she walked over and grabbed his hand. She pried open his fingers and removed her key from his grasp.

"This is about *you* getting what *you* want. And you'll do whatever it takes," she said through gritted teeth. "You'll lie to me, Becker. Manipulate me. Push everybody else out of my life. This is about *you* wanting to own me, and that is not love."

Faith thrust her key down into her pocket. Then she went over to the closet and pulled her out her fringed leather cowboy jacket.

"Where are you going?" he demanded.

"I'm going to the party. I need to talk to my friends right now," she muttered, patting her pockets to check for her wallet.

"I love you," Becker whispered. Then his voice rose. "I said I love you! Doesn't that mean anything to you? Don't you care about me at all?"

The intensity of his voice startled Faith and she watched his face twist into a white mask. Angry tears began streaming down his cheeks. Was he really hurt? Or was this some kind of act?

"I'll do something desperate," Becker threatened. "I don't know what. But I swear I'll do something desperate."

He turned and swiped his arm across her desk, violently knocking the piles of books and papers to the floor. Then he collapsed into her chair and put his head down on the surface. "You'll regret this. If you leave, I'll make you regret it. You'll be sorry," he sobbed.

Faith's eyes opened wide with disgust. She couldn't believe it. What a brat. Becker was actually having an infantile, stupid, hysterical *temper tantrum*. She wasn't going to give him what he wanted, and he was going to make her sorry? How lame could you get?

She was sorry already. Sorry she had ever given him the time of day. The self-possessed, intellectual, mature Becker Cain didn't exist, she realized. It was just an act. An illusion. The real Becker Cain was a clinging, possessive, emotional child. Faith had spent enough time around children to know that the best way to deal with a temper tantrum was to ignore it.

While Becker still had his head on her desk, Faith quietly left the room and started down the hall. As soon as he realized his audience was gone, he'd clear out, she figured. The door would lock automatically, so she didn't need to worry about that.

She shoved her hands down into her pockets and walked slowly toward the steps. A parade of old boyfriends marched across her memory. What a collection, she reflected sadly. Christopher had turned out to be a vain two-timing louse. Scott was a wild party guy who cared more about partying than he did about her. Elliot had cared about her, but he was married. Merideth cared very much about her, but he was gay. The parade passed by, and now Becker Cain brought up the rear.

Faith decided to let it pass. Right now, she needed to look ahead. She had to think what to do about the Professional Theater Program situation. What was she going to do?

At the bottom of the stairs, Faith broke into a run. She thought of her friends waiting for her at Winnie's. They were there for her. They would help her figure it out.

Lauren and Dash were talking in low tones in the dining alcove. Out of the corner of her eye, Lauren could see Brooks and Josh cleaning up the broken glass in the living room. She reached toward one of the plates of food, took a carrot stick, and nibbled it.

Lauren was glad that Faith hadn't been here for Melissa's outburst. It would have upset Faith a lot, and probably sent her running right back to Becker.

She wondered where Faith was, and if she was even coming.

She sighed, looked at Dash, then looked away again.

Things weren't turning out too well. Maybe it would be a good thing if Faith didn't come. Lauren sighed guiltily. It had been her idea to include Melissa. What a disaster that had turned out to be. Maybe she was just as wrong about dragging Faith over here for a get together with people she obviously felt ambivalent about.

Josh and Brooks were talking quietly as they searched the carpet for shards of glass. KC, Winnie, and Cody stood in another corner of the living-room, talking in hushed tones. The only people who seemed to have recovered quickly were Winnie's mother and her boyfriend. They sat on the living-room couch snuggling and talking together. After Melissa had left, Dr. Gottlieb had comforted Winnie. But after a few minutes, she had seemed to make a point of stepping to one side and letting Josh help Winnie pull herself together. Lauren concluded that Dr. Gottlieb was probably trying hard not to be an interfering mother-in-law.

There was a burst of laughter from the couch and Lauren saw Winnie throw a resentful look in her mother's direction. It wasn't the first time Lauren had seen her do it, either.

Lauren turned her attention back to Dash, who was still shaking his head over the scene. "I don't know Melissa that well," he was saying. "But her outburst seemed pretty out there."

"She took a real emotional beating at the altar," Lauren said quickly. "I don't think we should judge her too harshly."

"I'm not judging her," Dash protested. "All I said was that her behavior was out there, meaning not something you would expect someone to do." His flashing eyes softened immediately. "I'm sorry. Let's not argue."

Lauren pushed her glasses up. "Okay," she sighed. "Let's not. I'll even admit you're right. Melissa has gone through a pretty dramatic personality change recently. I thought it was just her feelings about the wedding coming to the surface, but now I'm beginning to wonder if there's more to the story."

Dash put his glass down on the table. "Now you're thinking. Maybe there's a story here. Maybe it's about the pressures of Olympic competition. How much competition is too much? How many athletes demonstrate personality changes as the pressure builds?"

"Is that how you see it?" Lauren asked, reaching for a another carrot stick and dipping it in the yogurt. "Is it a human-interest story? Or straight reporting?"

"It's your story, Turnbell-Smythe. You decide." He popped a cracker in his mouth and bit down hard, giving her a silly grin and making a loud crunch.

"My story?" Lauren exclaimed with her mouth full.

"Your story," he repeated after he swallowed the mouthful of cracker. He reached for a napkin and wiped his lips. "The story you could do for West Coast Woman Magazine. If you want to, I mean. Have you sent in your application?"

Lauren smiled. "You just gave it to me yesterday."

"Yeah. But you've got to jump on it. Get your pitch letter together tonight and attach it to the application." He popped another cracker in his mouth and munched it while he talked. "I'll help you. We'll look through your clips together. See which samples show you at your best."

He looked so excited and happy about helping her with the application that Lauren hated to disappoint him. But she had to make her feelings clear. She put her hand on his arm. "Dash," she said gently. "You're right. It's my story and I have to do it by myself. I have to fill out the application and send the samples by myself, too. I really appreciate your putting me on to this thing, but that doesn't mean I need you to help me with it."

"Need or want?" he asked. His eyelids looked down at the table but even his thick black lashes couldn't hide the hurt in his eyes. "I'm trying to be nurturing," he said seriously. "How can I nurture you if you won't let me?"

Lauren smiled. "I'm know you're trying and I appreciate it. But I've got to nurture myself right now. Learn to depend on myself. Maybe I did get a little carried away with the self-defense stuff and the feminism, but it doesn't change the fact that I don't want to be involved with you until I get straight on who I am and what I want."

"Okay. I understand," he said quickly.

She squeezed his arm and smiled softly. "I'm not sure if you do. And I'm sorry. But this is just the way it has to be."

Dash's shoulders slumped and his dark lashes lowered again. Then he leaned over and quickly kissed her cheek. "Okay. But call me when you get it all figured out." He started out of dining alcove. "You know my number."

"Dash," Lauren called after him. "Aren't you going to stay to watch Melissa's race on the television?"

He shook his head. "Nah. I need to figure out a few things, too."

# Sixteen

"Where have you been?" Terry demanded at the top of his voice.

"Something happened," Melissa panted as she jogged over to join the rest of the team. She darted a look up into the stands as she quickly began peeling off her jacket and sweatpants. The bleachers were filled to capacity, and men with television cameras balanced on their shoulders moved around the track, positioning themselves to get the best shots of the next race. "You told us not to be too early."

Terry snatched his hat off his head and threw it on the ground. "I also told you not to rush in here, either. You barely have enough time for your warm-up. What has gotten into you?"

Melissa couldn't believe it. She'd seen Terry get mad before, but she'd never seen him get this mad. Most of the time he was just doing it to scare them. But this time he really meant it. His face was red. His mouth trembled. Maybe the pressure had gotten to him.

Melissa didn't move.

"Don't just stand there. Start your warm-up!" Terry yelled.

She immediately bent over to stretch out the muscles in her back while he continued to lecture her.

"This is a team, Melissa. That means we have to be able to depend on each other. I have no room for loose cannons. And have no room for people who won't do it my way!"

Melissa bent her right knee and leaned over her left leg. "I'm sorry," she stuttered. What could she say? That she'd flipped out and tried to kill her ex-fiancé? And then after that she'd had to stop by her dorm room to take some illegal painkillers?

"Just start your warm-up and concentrate," he threatened. "You'd better run well, McDormand, that's all I can say." He shook his head, then moved a few yards away.

Melissa's face went scarlet with embarrassment.

The other 800-meter runners were trying to pretend they weren't watching and listening. But Melissa could feel them darting looks in her direction. She tried to ignore them and concentrate on her warm-up, running quickly through the bending and stretching exercises.

"First call for the women's 800!" blared the PA system a few minutes later.

She felt a hand clamp on her shoulder and she turned to see Terry's face looming over her again.

"What now?" she blurted. "I'm sorry, okay? I'm late. I had a terrible practice this week. But I'm going to win, Terry. I'm going to win!"

"I know you are," he said. "I'm sorry, Melissa. I shouldn't have come down on you like that. Not right before a race. I shouldn't have taken this out on you."

"Take what out on me?"

He took her arm and walked her away from the other runners. "Just because I'm mad at Bruneau doesn't mean I had a right to yell at you, even if you were a little late."

Melissa stopped. *Mad at Caitlin Bruneau?* What was he talking about? She'd missed Caitlin's race. Had Caitlin run poorly? "Didn't she place at all?" Melissa asked quickly.

A terrible look passed over Terry's face. "You didn't hear?"

Melissa shook her head. "Hear what?"

"They drug-tested the runners after the 400. Caitlin tested positive for steroids. She's been disqualified from this race and suspended from competition for a year."

Melissa's breath caught in her chest and an invisible fist punched her in the stomach. Poor Caitlin. How had she gotten caught? How horrible for Terry.

Terry patted her shoulder and faded into a crowd of coaches, runners, and television cameramen. "It's up to you to make us proud," she heard him say as two runners for the 800 streaked into lanes on either side of her, shaking their limbs and quivering like excited thoroughbred horses. "You can do it."

"Second call for the women's 800."

Four more runners positioned themselves in the staggered lanes along the starting line. Melissa's breath caught as a second invisible fist punched her in the stomach. If they'd tested the sprinters, they might test *everybody*. Caitlin had been using the same masking drug Melissa used. Caitlin always said that it wasn't an exact science. They were always mixing their drugs according to the latest theories and underground advice. Obviously this time the formula hadn't worked.

Terror slowed Melissa's heartbeat to a dull thud, and heavy dread coursed through her arms and legs.

If she got tested, she was finished. Her body was loaded with steroids, and, she suspected, probably some speed, too. On top of that, she had gulped down a mouthful of painkillers less than half an hour ago. What should she do? Drop out of the race now? She could say she was sick. She could say her tendon was bothering her.

"Runners, take your marks!" the loudspeaker squawked.

Automatically, she positioned her feet and took some deep breaths. She'd lose her chance to go to the Olympics if she defaulted. But it would be better than getting caught using illegal drugs and losing her scholarship. On the other hand, they might not test the middle-distance runners. She could still come through this and come out on top.

*It's a gamble, but it's your choice,* the bodybuilder had said.

So far, she'd gambled and won. Should she choose to gamble again?

Out of the corner of her eye, she saw something glinting in the sun. She couldn't keep her head from turning to look. Danny was sitting in his chair next to the bottom row of the bleachers, his hair shining almost white. The hair on her arms stood up and she knew that Danny's eyes were watching her and her alone.

Eventually, cheaters get caught.

"Crack!" went the starter's pistol.

The pack was off. Melissa hesitated in confusion for a split second, then her runner's instincts kicked in. She leaped forward. Her tense muscles uncoiled like springs, propelling her down the track and wiping every single thought from her mind except one— *Cross the finish line. And come in first.*

She pounded down the straightway and leaned slightly as she came around the curve. Then she pushed her legs into gear, slicing through the pack as soon as she saw a Western U runner pull out ahead and establish a firm lead.

She ran between the pack and the front-runner for awhile, then she poured on the speed, thrusting herself forward, passing the front-runner, and veering into her lane to cut her off.

She didn't see the runner's face, but she felt her desire as she passed her, and it produced a keen, sharp thrill in the base of her spine. The other runner's feet pounded behind her, determined to recapture her position. Melissa used her kick to run faster and . . .

"Ahhhh!" Melissa screamed.

Hot, searing pain pierced her ankle and sizzled up the back of her leg like a lit fuse. The pain was so horrible and frightening that her mind actually left her body and floated above the stadium.

She fell heavily to the ground, landing on her shoulder and bouncing slightly from the impact. Her head came up off the track, and then snapped around when the heel of the runner behind her connected with the side of her skull. Her hair spun slowly around her face like a halo, and a spray of perspiration flew out in a circular pattern.

Melissa's arms slowly rose to cover her head and her body began to roll toward the inside of the oval. Six more pairs of feet glided by her fallen body. The white toe of an athletic shoe kicked into Melissa's stomach, and her body curled protectively into a fetal position.

Her body began to roll in the other direction now—away from the oval toward the outer perimeter of the track. Then she lay motionless. Why was she lying there, she wondered? Didn't she have a race to run? The most important race of her life.

*Get up, Melissa. This is the pre-Olympic trial.*

She was relieved to get her body to move again. But something was wrong. She twitched and struggled. There was something wrong with her leg. She tried to get up, but the leg collapsed underneath her. This couldn't really be happening, could it? Not to Melissa. Not after all the hard work, and the drugs, and the pain. Couldn't somebody help her get up and run?

There were people on the track now. Two men were running to help her. But they weren't helping her to her feet. They were trying to get her off the track. *Let me run,* she wanted to shout.

One man started waving his hands and pointing. He was pointing at the pack.

The roar of the crowd reverberated through the stadium. Melissa's mind was suddenly back in her own body and the noise from the stands was deafening. Her leg was on fire and she could hardly breathe.

"Here they come," a voice yelled. "Get her off the track!"

Rough hands closed over her arms and legs and the next thing she knew she was being lifted across the rough surface of the clay track. She opened her eyes in time to see the pack thunder past on the last lap, their feet raising a red cloud.

She took a deep breath, and then gagged, choking on a mouthful of dry, red dust.

"No!" she screamed, as she realized that the race was completely and irretrievably lost. "Noooooo!"


Faith stood quietly behind the group gathered in front of the television. No one had seen her slip quietly in the front door a few minutes ago. They were glued to the pre-Olympic trials.

She had come in just in time to see Melissa's race, and now she squinted sadly at the picture on the screen. It showed a shot of some people hovering over Melissa on the sidelines. Faith thought she was probably the only person in this room who really could understand what Melissa was feeling right now. It was horrible to get that close to your dream, and then have it crumble.

Josh put his arm over Winnie's shoulder. "Poor Melissa! She had it in the bag, too. Some life, huh? One minute you're on top, the next minute you're on the bottom."

"Or out the door," Faith muttered.

All heads spun around. "Faith!" Winnie jumped to her feet and threw her arms around Faith.

KC stood and smiled. "Glad you made it."

"Sorry I'm late," Faith said with a rueful smile.

"Don't be sorry," Winnie said with a chuckle. "So far, it's been a really crummy party."

The guys on the floor all waved, then turned back to the TV. Brooks's eyes lingered on her face for a moment, then he gave her something that might have been a smile and looked back at the TV.

Lauren had been sitting next to Cody, but now she got up and stood slightly apart from the group. It was the way Faith remembered her at the beginning of their freshman year when she was always looking a little unsure of herself. Faith gave Lauren her warmest smile and Lauren smiled back with her violet eyes shining. Faith couldn't believe that she had actually let Becker come between her and her friends.

Just then, she caught sight of Dr. Gottleib standing in the dining alcove with a man. So that was the boyfriend. He seemed a little straight for Francine, but he looked pretty nice.

Faith squeezed Winnie's hand. "Let me just go over and say . . ."

Winnie's hand tightened over hers. "Mom can wait. Right now, we're going to be selfish and make you talk to us. This is a little awkward, but we're all really sorry we leaned on you so hard for so long. So now we're ready to be here for you for a change. If you'll let us."

Faith smiled. She sat down. "Good," she told them without hesitation. "Because I've got a big problem and I need you guys to listen and give me advice."

# Seventeen

"It sounds to me like you have two choices," Lauren told Faith. "One: You can play stupid. You don't know anything about the other production. Seattle? Where's that?"

Winnie and KC looked skeptical.

Faith propped herself up on her elbow. "What's my other choice?"

Lauren thought for a minute. The girls were all stretched out on Winnie and Josh's bed. It was just like old times, Faith reflected. She and Winnie and KC had been solving each other's problems like this since ninth grade. The only difference was that now they had Lauren, and Lauren had proved to be a very sensible sounding board.

"Go talk to the selection committee," Lauren suggested. "Tell them the truth and throw yourself on their mercy. Ask if you can reapply next year with another idea. All they can do is say no."

Faith put her braid in her mouth and moaned. "Along with a few other things, like *get lost* and *never darken our door again*. I won't have a friend left in the department."

Winnie patted her.

Tears stung Faith's eyes and she blinked hard trying to stop the flow. Theater people could be the most generous, giving, loyal, wonderful people in the world. But they could also be the harshest and most unforgiving critics. Merideth might stick by her, but everyone else would turn their backs on her. She wouldn't blame them. She had loved being part of the theater. She had adored the excitement, the friendships, and even the feuds. To be excluded from all that seemed like the worst fate in the world. She wasn't just going to be kicked out of the Professional Theater Program, she was going to be forced out of the whole theater community of the school.

Winnie reached out and put her hand on top of Faith's. "You'll have us, though. I promise. Whatever happens, we'll be behind you for a change."

KC put her hand down on top of Winnie's. "All for one."

Lauren smacked her hand down on top of KC's. "And one for all. It's time we stopped pulling in four different directions, and started pulling together."

Faith looked at KC and Winnie and Lauren and their faces gave her courage. "Okay," she gulped. "I think it's pretty clear what I have to do. I can't start my theater career on a stolen idea. Even if nobody ever found out about it, I would know and feel like a phony."

"So you're not going to play stupid?" KC grinned.

"I played stupid the day I fell for Becker Cain," Faith groaned. "He got me into this. But it doesn't matter. I'm perfectly capable of getting myself out of it. Monday morning, I'm going to call the department and ask to see the selection committee as soon as possible."

They were all quiet until Josh appeared at the doorway.

"Win." He had been coming in every few minutes to fill them in on the results of the trials and let them know whether or not there was any news about Melissa. "The trials are over. No more news on Melissa. Brooks and Dash just left."

Lauren and KC got up off the bed. "I've got to shove off, too," KC said.

"Me three," Lauren echoed.

"I'll walk with you guys," Faith said. She quickly

tugged on her cowboy boots and hurried out the bedroom door behind KC and Lauren.

The group trooped into the living room and Faith looked around. "Where's your mom?" she asked Winnie.

"She and Craig went out a little while ago to take a walk," Josh answered as he disappeared into the hall.

"Oh, no," KC and Faith moaned in unison.

"I'm sorry I didn't get to talk to her," Faith said. Winnie's mother was great, and Faith had always been fond of her. She noticed that Winnie's face looked unhappy and a little angry. "Is something wrong?" Faith asked her.

Winnie shook her head and gave Faith a little hug. "Nope," she answered quickly. "I'm just a moody pregnant lady."

Faith frowned at Winnie, trying to decide if she was telling the truth. Winnie reached for a long scarf that was draped over a chair and began waving it around her head. "Git along. Round 'em up and move 'em out. Yeehaaa, rawhide."

"We're going. We're going." KC laughed, pulling Faith and Lauren out the front door behind her.

"Bye, Moody Pregnant Lady," they all shouted as Winnie closed the door.

\* \* \*

Half an hour later, Winnie dropped a tray of dirty dishes on the counter. Right now, she felt like the moodiest, most unhappy pregnant lady in the world. Where was her mother? Couldn't she at least help them clean up? Her back was aching and all of her joints twinged with weird, sharp pains.

Finally, Winnie heard the front door slam and the sound of her mother's laughter drift toward the kitchen. "I took Craig over and showed him the campus. He's very impressed with the U of S facilities," her mother went on, walking over to the coffee pot and rummaging through the mess on the counter for a clean cup. "He says it reminds him of his old school."

"Isn't that nice," Winnie said sarcastically. Why was her mother talking about Craig? Did she really think Winnie was interested in hearing about some man she'd never laid eyes on until a few days ago?

"Winnie?" her mom said. "I know you're probably still upset about Melissa, but is there something else?"

Winnie dropped a handful of cups into the sink with a crash. "Yes. Now that you mention it, there is something else." She grabbed a dish towel and angrily dried her hands. "What's wrong is that you told me you were going to be here yesterday afternoon." She turned and saw her mother's surprised face. "You didn't show up. You didn't call. And you didn't let me know where you were until late yesterday evening."

"Winnie!" her mother laughed. "You knew I was with Craig."

"You're my mother!" Winnie shouted, feeling close to tears. "I was worried about you. What's the matter with you? You're just acting like some flaky teenager. Running off and disappearing with some guy. Doing whatever you feel like doing and not thinking about anybody but yourself. Didn't you even stop to think that I might need you?"

"Winnie. Why in the world shouldn't I do exactly what I want to do at this point in my life? You're all grown up and on your own. You don't need me anymore."

"Yes, I do!"

Her mother frowned. "Because you were having a party?"

"Because I'm having a baby!" Winnie yelled. "I'm pregnant!"

Someone coughed. Winnie looked up and saw Craig and Josh standing in the kitchen door.

Her mother looked stunned.

Josh glanced down at his feet and Craig flushed a deep pink.

"I'm sorry," Craig said quietly. "I didn't mean to intrude." He turned to Josh. "Why don't you and I go pick up some Chinese food for supper? Maybe Winnie and Francine would like to have some time alone."

"Sure," Josh said. He grabbed his jacket from

the back of a kitchen chair. "We'll be back later."

The men hurried out of the kitchen, and Winnie and her mother stared at the door for a long moment.

"You're having a baby?" her mother finally repeated.

Winnie nodded. At last, she had her mother's attention.

Her mom sighed. "Okay. Let's talk."

Francine took her coffee cup and went into the living room. Winnie walked behind her and they sat down on the couch. Winnie felt her anger begin to disappear. Maybe her mom would apologize now. Promise to be more responsible. She would ask Winnie how she could help. Things would start working out now.

Her mom took a sip of her coffee and swallowed thoughtfully.

"Well?" Winnie said. "Aren't you going to say anything?"

"What do you want me to say?" her mother asked. "That I'm thrilled? That I think it's a good idea? I can't say that, because I'm not thrilled and I'm not so sure it's a good idea. But it's your choice, so I accept it."

"Why do you always say that?" Winnie came back. "I didn't choose to get pregnant right now. But it happened anyway."

Her mom shrugged. "You're a smart girl, Win.

You know about birth control. I made sure you knew. Didn't you use any?"

"I did. Most of the time."

Her mother shook her head. "All it takes is one time. I can't change that reality for you. As much as I love you, want to protect you, and wish for you every good thing that life has to offer, that's just the way it is."

Winnie swallowed the lump that was rising in her throat. This wasn't going the way she planned. This didn't sound like the usual shrink-rap. This sounded like the splash of a bucket of cold water.

Her mom put her coffee cup down, then reached out and stroked Winnie's cheek. "The other fact of life is that children grow up and stop being children, Win. They lead their own lives. And they have to let their parents lead their own lives, too."

"But I'm part of your life, Mom!" Winnie protested with a sob, unable to believe that her mother was actually pulling away. "And I want you to be part of mine."

"I will be," her mother assured her. "But in a different way than I was when you were growing up. I'm not going to be in charge of your life anymore. I do have to think about my life. I'm in love, Winnie. Craig travels a lot and I want to be free to go with him. I'm trying to cut down on my patient load and other responsibilities so that I can have some time for myself, and time for him."

"What about time for me?" Winnie asked in a small voice.

Her mom took her hands. "I'll make time for you, too. I love you, Winnie. And once I get used to the idea, I'm probably going to love being a grandmother. But it's your baby. Your responsibility. You'll be the mother. You'll make the decisions. You'll be the grown-up."

Winnie wiped her nose. "I'm not sure I'm ready to be a grown-up," she whispered. "And I don't think I'm ready to be a mother, either."

Her mom sighed and drew Winnie's head down on her shoulder. "No one ever is. You'll play it by ear, Winnie. Just like I did. Nothing ever happened the way I expected it to. Career, marriage, or motherhood. But somehow, I got through it. And so will you."

This was it, Winnie realized with a sinking heart. This was the best she was going to get from her mother. There weren't going to be any whoops of joy or shrieks of excitement. No plans. No suggestions. No enthusiastic schemes for making Winnie's life easier. Her mom was making it pretty clear that she and Josh were on their own with this baby. She was acknowledging that Winnie was an adult. Winnie felt absolutely terrified.

# Eighteen

"**H**ow bad is it?" Melissa asked fearfully.

The pain in her Achilles tendon had calmed down somewhat, but it was still throbbing. After her fall, it had taken Melissa several minutes to come to her senses. But as soon as her head stopped ringing, four runners from the men's team had carried her across the parking lot to the massage room of the Athletic Complex. There they'd sent for the university Health-Center doctor who treated all the athletes.

The doctor had told her he couldn't tell anything until the initial swelling subsided. So she had been sitting on the massage table with an ice pack around her ankle for an hour and a half now.

The doctor removed the ice pack, took it over to the sink, and dropped it in. "I'm going to take another look now," he said, coming back over to the table.

Melissa shivered. The room was so cold. And it didn't offer much in the way of comfort. It had two massage tables, a white porcelain-and-chrome sink area, and a variety of sports-medicine paraphernalia stored on a long counter that ran the length of one wall.

The doctor gently ran his fingers over her tendon.

She flinched. Her whole ankle was sore to the touch.

"How bad is it?" she repeated. Maybe the damage wasn't too terrible. Maybe he would just give her some linament and tape and tell her to take it easy for a few days.

"I can't imagine what happened," she chattered nervously, trying to minimize it in her own mind, and the doctor's. "I don't know what made the tendon hurt so bad all of a sudden. It's probably just one of those freak things that happens every once in a while."

"I treated you for this tendon last fall," the doctor said after a long pause. "And I can tell by the way this feels that it's been bothering you for a while. This is not a new injury. Let's not kid each other. There's only one way you could have gotten through the pain and kept running on it, and that's steroids or painkillers. Or both."

Melissa wanted to jump off the examining table and run.

The doctor saw her body tense and he put a restraining hand on her shoulder. "Don't panic. I'm not going to recommend a drug test. You didn't finish the race and there aren't any meet results to dispute. Under the circumstances, I don't see any reason to ruin your college athletic future. What's left of it," he added with a shake of his head.

"You mean . . ." Melissa's lips began to tremble.

"This tendon is partially torn. Seriously injured," he barked impatiently.

"But what does that mean?" she cried. "Are you saying it's injured permanently?"

"I'll get to that in a minute. But first I want you to listen to me."

He sat down on a stool with tiny wheels on the bottom and rolled toward the table until his face was inches from hers. "You are taking a very dangerous and very stupid risk when you use those drugs. They can damage your liver, your reproductive system, and other organs, too. It's not worth it, Melissa. No scholarship or gold medal is worth the price if the price is your health."

Melissa couldn't look at him.

"Enough of that lecture for a minute," he went on. "Let's talk about pain. It's not just something to get over or ignore for the sake of being stoic. Pain is your body's way of telling you something's wrong. Your body was trying to tell you to ease up on your leg.

You didn't listen. You tried to cover up the pain and keep going and the result is . . ."

Melissa closed her eyes, mentally pleading with him not to say it.

". . . you may have injured the tendon permanently." His hand squeezed her shoulder. "I'm sorry."

Her whole body began to shake. *Injured permanently* meant she was through. No more running. No more scholarship, either. What else was there?

"You need crutches," the doctor continued. "I'll find somebody to take you over to the Health Center so you can be fitted for a pair. I don't want you to take one single step on that leg, not for a week or two."

As his footsteps echoed down the corridor, her chin fell down onto her chest. She clenched her teeth tight. Everything hurt now. Her ankle. Her head. But most of all, her heart. That was the worst pain of all. The dull, slow, sickening, throbbing ache of disappointment, humiliation, and regret.

*It's a gamble, McDormand.*

Melissa had gambled, and had lost everything she prized in one moment. The race. Her shot at the Olympics. Her spot on the team. Her friends. Her self-respect. And maybe her scholarship and her entire future.

A silent tear trickled down her cheek. She felt a second tear forming. Melissa jerked her hand to her face and fiercely wiped it away.

"I'm sorry," she suddenly heard a deep voice say.

Slowly, Melissa lifted her head.

Danny had just wheeled into the open doorway. Slowly he came over and joined her at the table. His green eyes were softer and sadder than she had ever seen them.

Melissa tried to stop her tears, but they kept falling down her face.

"I've been waiting for you," he explained. "I saw the race and I thought you might need a ride somewhere." His upper body moved slightly forward as he spoke. "I just heard the doctor say you needed a ride to the Health Center."

Her lip began to tremble and she bit down on it. She didn't want to cry in front Danny, or anybody else. Every disastrous thing that had happened today was her own fault. She might not have been much of a sportswoman in the past, but she could start being one now.

"You going to be okay?" he asked softly.

There was something about his face. The way he had to turn it up to look at her from where he sat. She had never seen such genuine, sweetly expressed concern in her life. And it made it seem okay to cry. Her chest heaved and her shoulders shook as she really began to sob.

He held up his arms. "Come on. Let's get you over to the Health Center. Get on my lap."

"I . . . I can't," she sobbed. "I'll . . . fall . . . or I'll hurt you."

"No, you won't," he promised. "Come on," he coaxed.

Melissa eased herself off the table and Danny's muscular arms reached up and skillfully pulled her into his lap. Melissa's arms encircled his neck and his arms tightened around her.

"It's over," she wept into his solid shoulder. "My life is over." She felt the muscles of his arms ripple against the skin of her back as he held her even tighter.

"No, it's not," he whispered. "I know you think it is. But it's not."

"You don't understand," she wept.

He laughed softly and rested his cheek against the top of her head. "I think I do."

"But you can draw. It's different for me. Running is all I ever had," she choked. "If I can't run, I don't know who I am anymore."

He pushed the mop of damp hair back off of her forehead. "Then it's time to find out, isn't it?" He smiled, and Melissa felt her heart go flip-flop when she realized how close his face was to hers. His skin was absolutely flawless, and she felt the golden tips of his eyelashes flutter against her cheek.

He drew back his head and smiled again. "Now, if the crying portion of the day is finished, I suggest we roll."

Melissa swayed slightly as his arms began to move the wheels. "Are you sure this is going to work?" she asked, tightening her grip around his shoulders.

"Trust me," he said, skillfully navigating through the doorway.

The hallway was empty and he turned left when they reached the corner. "The front door is the other way," she said.

"But the ramp is at the side door," he smiled. "Ever been on a roller coaster?"

"Yes," she said nervously. "Why?"

"Well, that's nothing compared to The Ramp. Believe me, you haven't lived until you've traveled down a ninety-degree incline in a wheelchair going fifty miles an hour."

She wiped her tears again. "This wheelchair won't do fifty."

"Well, not in town," he admitted. "But on the highway . . . "

She tried to laugh. "You can't scare me."

The side door was propped open and she saw the ramp. Her stomach lurched and she held on to Danny for dear life as the wheelchair coasted down the steep ramp and onto the paved walkway. It wasn't a ninety-degree incline, but it felt like it.

The fresh air made her feel a little better. A cool breeze ruffled through her hair and blew back the front strands of Danny's hair. His arms continued to push, and his eyes watched the walkway for obstacles. His glance dropped for a moment to meet her eyes and she flushed, realizing she had been caught staring.

"Melissa," he began. "I know we didn't get off to a good start the other day. And I probably didn't express myself too well about the steroids. But . . ."

"You don't have to say anything," she said quickly. "I've gotten the lecture and I've learned my lesson. Not that it makes any difference now. My running days are probably over."

"Come on, Mel. You don't know that yet."

"I don't know anything anymore," she said, her voice catching as her misery welled up all over again.

He stopped the chair and put his arms around her, pulling her head down until it rested in the crook of his neck. She felt the beat of his heart and the warmth of his chest.

"Nobody ever sees the future," he whispered in her ear. "Nobody ever knows what's going to happen next, good or bad. That's why it's important to enjoy things while you can. So right now, why don't you just relax, enjoy the view, and leave the driving to us. Okay?"

"Okay." She managed a smile. Suddenly, she was exhausted. All the stress, the painkillers, the tears, and the disappointment welled up. She rested her head against Danny's neck, content to let go of the worry for a moment.

The chair rocked slightly as it made its way across campus. They passed the Administration Office, the

Student Union, and from time to time, when she opened her eyes, she saw a few heads turn to look curiously at the sight of a guy in a wheelchair crossing the campus with a girl in his lap.

Before she knew it, they were rolling up the wheelchair ramp and into the front door of the Health Center. "Have you ever been on crutches before?" he asked her.

Melissa shook her head as they approached the check-in desk. "No. Is it hard to walk with them?"

"I'm told they can take some getting used to. I'd better wait and follow you back to your dorm in case you have trouble with them."

"Melissa McDormand?" A uniformed nurse hurried toward them, pushing an empty wheelchair. "The doctor told us to expect you. We've got some crutches for you to try in the examining room." She took Melissa's arm. "Get in this wheelchair and I'll take you in."

Melissa hated to leave the warmth of Danny's lap. But she was too tired to resist as the nurse pulled on her arm. "I don't know how long I'll be," she said to Danny as she transferred to the other wheelchair and sat down.

Danny leaned forward and took her hand. She felt gentle pressure on the tips of her fingers. He shook his head as she got into a chair of her own. "It doesn't matter," he replied softly. "I'll be here."

# Nineteen

"*I* gave her the application. I suggested a story. I offered to help her put it all together. She says thanks. Then she gives me a long speech about how she's got to find out who she really is and asks me to back off for a while." Dash swung his arm around in a modified version of a pitcher's windup and tossed a tennis ball across the dorm room.

Brooks caught it easily from his desk chair. "So?"

"So I backed off. Decided to wait it out. But it's been days now, and she hasn't called me or anything. How long does it take somebody to figure out who they are?" he asked irritably.

"What are you going to do?" Brooks tossed the ball back to Dash.

Dash caught it and held on to it, squeezing it with his hand. "I thought maybe I'd go back to the Men's Support Group," he answered shyly. "That's why I dropped by. I thought you might want to come with me."

Brooks smiled. "You're really into that stuff now, huh?"

Dash felt his ears turning red. He was afraid this was going to happen. "Don't laugh!" he warned.

"I'm not laughing," Brooks laughed.

Dash playfully tossed the ball at Brooks, pretending to aim it right at him. "I told you not to laugh."

The ball flew slightly off course and Brooks twisted his body to pluck the ball out of the air. It landed in Brooks's broad palm with a soft thump and Dash couldn't help envying the easy grace Brooks seemed to have when it came to physical stuff.

Dash knew he projected a certain amount of machismo, but he'd always been more cerebral than athletic. He and Baldwin were completely different types. But in the important ways, they were alike. They were two masculine guys who genuinely wanted to get along with the opposite sex, but just couldn't figure out how to do it.

"Look," Dash said, fumbling the catch as Brooks

lobbed the ball back. "I know that neither one of us got any foolproof pointers for getting along with women . . ."

"I'll say," Brooks exclaimed, rolling his eyes. "Look what happened to me. I tried to do something nice for Melissa and she almost killed me. The sensitive and giving approach is obviously not what works for her."

"But if enough guys like us put their heads together, maybe we can come up with some answers that make sense. All I know is I can't just sit around doing nothing. The Men's Support Group is the only thing I can think of to do."

"I feel exactly the same way. I can't sit around doing nothing either." Brooks stood up and grabbed his knapsack.

"Then you'll come to the meeting?"

"No. But I'll walk over to the Student Union with you. I've got an appointment there."

Dash stood and hoisted his own knapsack. "Good. It's a ten-minute walk. That gives me ten minutes to talk you into coming to the meeting with me."

A veil seemed to come down over Brooks's face and he lost some of his animation. "You'll be wasting your breath."

"I've got a lot of breath," Dash said as they left the room. "I don't mind wasting a little of it for a good cause."

Dash started talking a mile a minute as soon as they were outside. He argued persuasively and passionately. As they passed the sculpture garden, he pointed out that guys needed to learn to communicate with each other on a more intimate level. Outside McClaren Plaza, he pointed out the number of successes, innovations, and sheer miracles that had been achieved by collaborations of men with common goals. He invoked the Wright Brothers, the Ringling Brothers, the Marx Brothers, and by the time the Student Union came into view, he was even invoking the Smith Brothers.

"The operative word here," he said, "is *brothers*. Are you following me, Baldwin?"

He was breathless by the time they cut across the grass toward the concrete walk that led to the front steps of the Student Union. But he wished it had been a longer walk. Ten minutes wasn't turning out to be enough time. He was a fast talker, but Brooks didn't seem to be a fast thinker.

Brooks's face had that stolid, jock expression on it that reminded Dash of a water buffalo. Or an elephant. Was he even listening?

"It's a confusing world, Baldwin," Dash said as they climbed the front steps of the Student Union.

"Very confusing," Brooks agreed absently.

"Men today need direction."

"Uh huh."

"Men today need guidance."

"Yup."

"Men today want to do the right thing, but we don't know what it is. So we need guidelines."

"You're right," Brooks nodded. He pulled the heavy glass door open and let Dash walk in first.

"So are you coming to the meeting?"

"Nope." Brooks let the door close behind him.

The Student Union was crowded. Students hurried in every direction, streaming in and out of the bookstore and cafeteria. "Last chance," Dash smiled, holding out his arms and giving Brooks a comic, used-car-salesman smile.

Brooks smiled enigmatically and shook his head. "I can't. I've got an appointment."

Dash lifted his shoulders in a disappointed shrug. He'd given it his best shot. "Then I guess I'll see you around."

Brooks nodded, but he didn't wander away. Dash was surprised when Brooks continued to walk beside him, following him up the stairs to the second floor where the university offices and club meeting rooms were located. "Where's the appointment?"

Brooks stopped outside a door, and gestured toward it with his chin. "In there."

Dash stared blankly for a minute, his eyes studying the poster on the door. Some macho guy in a uniform with an eagle behind him. Suddenly, Dash understood and his eyes practically bulged in their sockets. "ROTC? You can't be serious."

Brooks nodded. "I picked up the information last week."

"Don't you think that's a little drastic?"

"I've given it a lot of thought," Brooks said quietly. He put his hand on the doorknob. "It's not right for everybody. But I think it's right for me."

"Hold it!" Dash grabbed Brooks's arm and tried to yank him back into the hallway. But Brooks stood firm. Dash held on anyway. "You can't do it, Baldwin. It's nuts. It's the ultimate commitment. They'll tell you what to wear. Tell you what to do. Tell you what to think."

Brooks calmly reached over and detached Dash's fingers from his sleeve. "I know."

Dash fell back and they stared at each other for a moment. He *was* wasting his breath, Dash realized. Brooks lifted his square jaw, and suddenly he didn't look like a water buffalo anymore. Or an elephant.

He looked like a man with his mind made up.

Faith couldn't believe the time had finally come. But mixed with the sense of dread that was making her feet feel like lead was a sense of relief. She had

had to wait to get an appointment with the Professional Theater Group Selection Committee. She was anxious to get it over with. No matter what happened now, it couldn't be worse than the anticipation. For days, she'd hardly been able to eat, or sleep, or concentrate on anything else.

The white, high-ceilinged hallways of the Theater Arts Building were covered with thick red carpet. Her feet made no noise in the silent corridor and she realized that the steady rhythmic sound she heard was the beating of her own frightened heart. By the time she reached Rehearsal Room B, she was shaking.

Faith smoothed her French braid and tucked the shirttail of her embroidered white cotton blouse into the waistband of her denim skirt. Then, summoning every ounce of courage she possessed, she knocked softly.

"Enter," a voice called out.

Faith opened the door and walked in. Five pairs of curious eyes fastened on her face. The Professional Theater Group Selection Committee members sat around an oval conference table piled high with scripts and dotted with coffee cups. The walls of the room were dark, and the table was lit with lamps that hung from the ceiling.

She recognized some of the faces from the department. But she recognized Dr. Bruce Walling's face from her theatre magazines. He was an international legend. A tall, elegant Englishman in his late sixties, and one of the foremost playwrights of the century.

He'd come to U of S last year to serve as Playwright in Residence and conduct an honors writing seminar for graduate students. Faith contemplated the awful humiliation of admitting her theft in front of such an eminent member of the theater community.

Dr. Walling stood and motioned to an empty chair. "Please sit down, Ms. Crowley."

Faith sat, darting a nervous look at the other members of the selection committee.

The other four members of the committee sat forward and peered intently at her through their glasses. They all wore black turtlenecks, and it made their faces look like four ghostly masks floating eerily against the dark backdrop of the walls.

Faith shrank a little in her seat.

Dr. Walling smiled. "I'm not quite sure why you asked to see us. But let me begin by telling you again how terribly impressed we all were with your proposal for a wild west *Taming of the Shrew*." He tapped his fingers on the red folder in front of him, which Faith recognized as her proposal.

"Actually," Faith squeaked, her voice sounding high and tinny. "That's what I wanted to talk to you about."

She took a deep breath, and then explained as clearly and as concisely as she could that the idea for her proposal had been based on the suggestion of a friend. And that subsequent to the presentation of her proposal, it had come to her attention that the same idea had been in used in the 1977 Seattle Shakespeare Festival production. By the time she finished talking, her mouth was as dry as the desert and her armpits were soaking wet.

"That's all I have to say," Faith said softly. "Except that I didn't mean to do it, and I'm sorry."

There was a long pause and then . . . Dr. Walling chuckled. Soon just about everyone around the room was laughing or smiling.

Faith couldn't believe it. Were they crazy? Did they always laugh when they were getting ready to throw somebody out of the program?

Dr. Walling coughed into a handkerchief, trying to compose himself. "Forgive us, Ms. Crowley." His eyes twinkled. "We really shouldn't laugh. But sometimes we cannot help being amused by the . . . er . . . innocence of some of our students."

"I said I was sorry," Faith managed.

"Don't be sorry. There's nothing to be sorry for." He tapped his finger on the red cover of her proposal. "Let me hasten to assure you that you've done nothing wrong. You're not the first director to envision a wild west version of *The Taming of the Shrew*. And I think it's probably accurate to say you won't be the last."

"I . . . don't understand."

"Let us say there are only twenty-nine stories in the world. Everything else is just a variation on those themes. There's no such thing as a truly original notion. Even Shakespeare had inspiration for his plots. You're just participating in an old and time-honored theater tradition. What's important is taking an old idea and turning it into something new. Or taking an idea that doesn't work and turning it into something that works very nicely indeed. And that, Ms. Crowley, is exactly what you've done!"

He gestured around the table. "Every one us in this room saw that 1977 production in Seattle. It was abysmal. But this? Ahhhhh," he breathed. "Now *this* looks promising. You actually solved the problems of the production. And quite creatively, I might add."

It was all Faith could do not to jump across the table and throw her arms around Dr. Walling.

"Do you have anything else you'd like to tell us?" he asked, waving his glasses again. "If not . . ." He trailed off and gestured toward the pile of scripts on the table with his hand, indicating that they had work to do.

She stood, collecting her book bag and purse. "No, sir," she stuttered. "Just thanks and . . . and . . ." She laughed. ". . . and a million more thanks."

Dr. Walling laughed, and as she hurried out the door, she felt like a death-row prisoner who had just received an eleventh-hour pardon.

Outside the door, she opened her mouth and let out a silent scream of joy. She danced down the hallway toward the lobby of the building. And when she reached the lobby, she twirled happily underneath the large chandelier that hung from the vaulted ceiling. Over to the left were a pair of heavy, leatherpaneled doors studded with brass nails. The student theater was behind those doors. Faith couldn't resist taking a peek. Next year, she thought gleefully, she would be directing in that theater.

Faith pirouetted toward the doors like the heroine of an MGM musical. Then she pulled the heavy doors open and stepped inside. Up on the stage of the dark theater, she recognized an exotic-looking girl from the art department, painting clouds and stars on a scrim that would be used in an upcoming production.

As she walked down the center aisle, something in the left-hand aisle seat caught her attention. When she looked closer, she saw that it was a face. A very familiar face.

"Becker!"

His face looked startled and guilty and Faith realized that he had probably been following her, and then wandered in here while she was in the conference room. It was on the tip of her tongue to tell him off, but then she felt a rush of guilt. He might be a possessive nuisance, but if it hadn't been for him, she wouldn't be in the Professional Theater Group. Whether he realized it or not, he had been right about borrowing the idea. She remembered his anguished tears and decided that she did owe him something—at least a good-bye.

"I'm glad you're here," she said in low tone. "I just wanted to let you know that I saw the Selection Committee and everything is going to be all right. So I'm sorry I was so hard on you."

"Faith," he began, his face taking on a peculiar look.

"But you can't follow me around," she continued. "No room keys. No studying together. No relationship at all. Sorry. We're still finished."

"Faith," he tried to interrupt.

"It's not any fun for me to have to hurt you," she said gently but firmly. "But you have to understand that as much as you may think you love me, I don't love you back."

Just then the exotic-looking girl from the art department hopped down from the stage and came walking up the aisle. She was wearing paint-spattered overalls. Long dark hair fell to her waist, and her lips were a funky red. She gave Becker a radiant smile, and when he stood, she immediately put a possessive arm around his waist.

"Who is this?" the girl asked, looking at Faith. Her

red lips were smiling, but Faith saw a dangerous glint in her eye.

"Cheryl, this is an old friend, Faith," Becker explained quickly, placing the emphasis on the word *friend*. He turned to Faith. "Cheryl and I met at the film festival I went to while you were at Winnie's party."

Her face turned pouty and her fingers closed over the waistband of his baggy slacks. Without saying another word, the girl began to propel Becker up the aisle toward the doors. "Let me make something clear, Becker," Faith could hear her say as they left. "I don't like competition. From anybody. If you're with me—you're with me. And only me."

Faith plopped down in a seat and stared at the empty stage in stunned amazement. Only a short time before, he had been sobbing his eyes out in her room. Now here he was with a new girl. A very possessive new girl. A girl who was making it clear that she would accept nothing less than Becker's undivided attention.

Faith's lips twitched, and then her shoulders began to shake. She slapped her knee and one cowboy boot stomped the floor. Soon, the empty theater echoed with peals of her laughter.

They were *perfect* for each other.

# Twenty

*M*elissa stumped out of the Health Center on her crutches. *Wait and see,* the doctor had said. *It hasn't even been a week.* There was nothing to do now but stay off the leg, go on with her routine, and hope for the best.

It was hard to go on with her routine, though. Everything felt so up in the air. Her scholarship was good until the end of the year. But after that, if she couldn't run, she'd have to figure out some other way to finance her education.

Time had hung heavy on her hands over the last several days. Not being on the track team anymore left her with a lot of empty hours to fill. She was bored.

She was lonely. She was worried. She was feeling empty and low-energy as her body withdrew from the steroids. But most of all, she was feeling disappointed. It had been almost a week since Danny had followed her back to her dorm, helped her into bed, and then sat beside her while she cried herself to sleep. He'd been gone when she woke up and she hadn't seen or heard from him since.

KC, Winnie, and Faith had all dropped by within a few days after the race. Melissa had apologized for her behavior at Winnie's. But it was going to take some time to get over the awkwardness between them all.

Lauren had been pretty nice and understanding. And Melissa had done her best not to be irritable or grumpy. Maybe they would actually wind up friends again. She had gotten cards and flowers from her teammates. Caitlin had come by and they had commiserated with each other over their mutual bad luck.

But she hadn't heard one word from Danny, and she didn't know what to think.

Melissa stumped across the campus, enjoying the sun and the air. She'd been spending a lot of time in bed and it was nice to be out. Nice to be in civilian clothes, too. She had spent every waking minute for so long in track clothes. Today she wore a full skirt and blouse in a warm green that brought out the russet of her hair and the color of her cheeks and lips.

Lauren had smilingly asked her if she had a crush on her doctor when Melissa had left the dorm for her appointment. Why else would Melissa take the trouble to look so nice?

Melissa had laughed and remarked on the doctor's good looks. But she didn't tell her there was someone else she hoped to see.

And finally she saw him.

As she passed the art building she saw his chair parked on the grassy lawn in front. His head was bent over his lap and she could tell that he was drawing. Should she stop and talk? Or just pass on by? But even as her mind was debating, the crutches were carrying her across the grass.

If it hadn't been for Danny, she never would have gotten through the day of the race. She needed at least to thank him for that.

His hair hung down his back and he was wearing a blue tank top and a blue bandanna headband. As she approached, she noticed how the tanned muscular shoulders moved slightly as he drew. The thick grass muffled the sound of her crutches and she was able to move right behind him and look over his shoulder without his knowing she was there.

Danny's hand wielded the pencil with swift, sure strokes. A thick line. A thin one. A squiggle. Like magic, a picture of the university library in its wooded setting began to emerge on the page.

"Are you supposed to be up and around?" he asked, not turning around.

"How did you know I was behind you?" she asked in surprise.

He laughed. "I have supernatural powers." He gestured toward the library building with his pencil. "And besides, I saw your reflection in the plate-glass window over there."

Melissa laughed and stumped around the chair. "I'm glad I ran into you," she said. "I wanted to thank you for helping me on the day of the race."

Danny looked up from his work and met her gaze squarely. His eyes had lost the frank and open look she had seen on the day of the race. They looked the way they had the day they talked on the green—when he had given her the cartoon. They looked interested, but also a little defensive. A little antagonistic. And today, even a little angry. "Glad I could be of service," he responded.

She blushed and felt confused. Something had changed between them since the day of the race. What was the matter with him all of a sudden? "It's nice for the handicapped to feel useful now and then."

Melissa blinked, surprised by the edge in his voice. How was she supposed to respond to a statement like that? He was watching her closely, waiting for her to say something. But it was just like the day in the gym. Her mind was blank and she didn't know what to say.

"This is a big problem for you, isn't it?" He slapped his hands against the wheels of the chair.

Her mouth opened and then closed again. Was it? She wasn't sure. All she knew was that she had wanted to see him again. Wanted to tell him how much his help had meant to her. But now that she'd found him, she felt shy and embarrassed and annoyed that he was putting her on the spot.

He closed the pad with a snap and put his pencils in a pouch. "Don't sweat it," he said abruptly. "If I were you, it'd be a problem for me, too. See you around."

"Wait!" she cried.

But the wheelchair was moving away.

Melissa moved her crutches into place and hurried after him. "Wait!"

The wheelchair kept going.

"Danny!"

But Danny's arms kept pushing the wheels, the muscles flexing as he worked to move the chair across the grass and bump it up onto the paved walkway.

"You're not being fair!" she yelled angrily.

The chair stopped. He turned.

Melissa stumped toward the chair, breathing hard with the effort. "I said, you're not being fair."

Danny cocked his head. "Stop me if you've heard this one before—but *life is not fair*." He put his hands to the wheels and started to turn.

"Hold it right there!" Melissa exploded.

He turned back.

She moved closer. "I'll tell you what I've got a problem with," she fumed. Anger was blowing the confusion away, and now she had plenty to say. "The problem is not the wheelchair. The problem is that you didn't call me. I thought I was going to hear from you. And I never did. I've had enough of guys who act like they're going to be there for me and then fade."

He threw out his hands in a gesture of frustration and anger. "Well, I didn't know whether you'd want to hear from me. You and I sort of made a connection the day of your race. But life had just dropped a big anvil on your head. I know firsthand how vulnerable that makes you. The day I woke up in a hospital bed with no feeling from the waist down, I thought no one would ever want to have anything to do with me again. Then this pretty nurse came in and smiled at me. I was so pathetically grateful, I would have cut my right arm off for her. I didn't call you because I don't want gratitude like that from you."

"Well, if you keep this up," she barked, feeling too angry to be embarrassed anymore, "you're not going to get any."

His green eyes looked amused for a moment, and then turned hostile. "I don't want pity from you, either."

Melissa's eyes narrowed. "I don't have time to feel sorry for you. I'm too busy feeling sorry for myself right now. In case you haven't noticed, I've got a few problems of my own!" she finished with a shout.

It broke the tension and he let out a reluctant laugh. He rubbed his fingers thoughtfully over his smooth jaw. "I guess you do at that," he muttered.

She stumped a little closer, feeling her full skirt twirl around her legs as the breeze blew across the grass. "I know I can never really understand what it's like for you. But I know what it's like to feel angry. And I know what it's like trying to deal with people's pity."

A look of wounded pride flashed across his handsome face, and Melissa felt her heart breaking. It wasn't pity that made her chest ache for him. It was understanding. He had been an athlete, just like her. Self-sufficient. Confident. Another overachiever.

Melissa let her body hang from the crutches. She ran a hand through her hair and then she began to talk. She told him about Brooks and how horrible and worthless being dumped had made her feel. She told him about the need to win, and the steroids, and the rages and the tears. She told him about what the doctor had said. And she told him how frightened, worried, and uncertain she felt about her future.

His eyes never left her face. Once or twice, his upper body inched forward, and a couple of times his hands gripped the wheels of his chair.

When she finished, he said nothing for a long time. Then he ran a hand through his hair and exhaled. "Sounds like we've got a thing or two in common," he breathed. He rolled his head around on his neck and Melissa saw the cords of his shoulders and throat tighten. "So where do we go from here?" he said.

"We could start with a cup of coffee at the Student Union."

Danny moved the drawing pad off of his lap and shoved it into the backpack that hung from the handles. Then he turned back to face her. "Want a ride?" He was smiling, but his green eyes flickered uncertainly.

Melissa stumped over, and then carefully lowered herself into his lap, feeling a little uncertain herself. She leaned the crutches against the side of the chair.

"Comfortable?"

She bit her lip. "I'm really not sure," she whispered honestly.

"Me, neither," he said softly.

They stared at each other for a moment. Then Melissa closed her eyes and felt his lips press against hers. Soft, sweet, and warm. She relaxed against his chest and ran her hand along the tight silky skin of his cheek.

His arms tightened, her arms flew around his neck, and she turned until she was pressed as closely against his chest as she could manage.

*Nobody knows what's going to happen next,* he had said, *good or bad.*

The future was uncertain. For everybody. But for now, it was enough to sit in Danny's lap and feel his arms around her. For now, it was enough to feel the beating of his heart against hers.

He was here. So was she. And that was enough. For now.

*Here's a sneak preview of*
**Freshman Heat,** *the twenty-fifth*
*book in the* **FRESHMAN DORM**
*series.*

T he skinheads poured out of the basement of Tri Beta house. "Oh, no!" Dash
gasped.

From his place in the dark shade of a weeping
willow tree at the side of the house, Dash could see a
basement window swinging on its hinges. Obviously,
the skinheads had forced it and gotten into the sorority
house. Dash must have shown up just minutes later.
The whole time he'd been running around looking
for them and wondering if they'd even show, they'd
been inside the place, soaking it with gasoline.

He saw smoke curling out the open basement window. Then he heard a crashing sound. Billy Jones

had lobbed a flaming bottle of gasoline at a second story window. It missed its mark, however, and crashed on the windowsill.

*Craashhhhhhhh.* From the sound, Dash knew that one of the skinheads had thrown another firebomb through one of the living room windows. Then Dash heard another.

People poured out onto the lawn, pushing, screaming and crying. Dash knew there must be scores of people still trapped inside.

*It's happening,* Dash realized. *The nightmare is coming true!* He had to stop the fire. He had to put it out, before flames enveloped the building, killing dozens.

"Lauren!" he screamed as he took off toward the open basement window and squeezed inside.

A blast of smoke and intense heat hit him square in the face. Nonetheless, he battled his way into the basement. Through the whirling smoke, Dash could make out flames curling up one wall. The fire was still manageable. He could put it out. He pulled off his T-shirt and began beating the flames with it. He put out a small section, but the fire had spread down the far side of the wall. A small bottle of gasoline stood near a pile of soaked rags. The fire edged closer and closer.

*An unexploded firebomb!* Dash gasped. He grabbed it just before the flames would have reached it and sent it up in a blazing inferno. *Evidence!* Dash thought. The police could use it to put Billy and his gang away for good.

Dash took in a big lungful of smoke and choked. His eyes burned. His head spun dizzily. He felt as if he was going to pass out from the heat. Flames exploded along a second wall. He was losing his battle against the fire.

*Get out of here!* Dash told himself. But fire had already enveloped the open window. Dash ran up the stairs. His lungs pleaded for clean air. Sweat poured down his neck. He turned the handle of the door. It was locked.

*Bamm, bamm, bamm.* Dash threw his body against the door. Below him, fire was edging up the steps.

*Bamm, bamm, bamm.* But no one heard.

But Dash could feel the door weakening. He threw himself against it again, and the door came splintering off its hinges. Dash fell headfirst into the kitchen. The unexploded firebomb was still in his hand.

Down the corridor and through the whirling smoke, Dash could make out a huge crowd pushing around the front door. People at the back of the crowd were screaming and crying hysterically that they wouldn't get out.

"Lauren!" Dash half-sobbed. She wasn't in the crowd.

"Come on!" Dash screamed at the people shoving

and yelling at the front door. "There's a back exit!"

No one heard him over the roar of the flames and the panicked yells. Dash ran toward the crowd, pulling on people to get them to listen.

"This way! Out the back."

He led half a dozen down the hallway and outside to safety. He dropped his scorched T-shirt and the firebomb evidence in a pile on the grass. Shirtless and without the firebomb now, he started back into the house to save more lives. But before he got there, the porch in the back went up in flames. No one was getting out that way any more.

Dash's chest heaved with sobs. The skinheads had won. They'd destroyed the Tri Beta house. A deep, frightened exhaustion enveloped Dash. He had a terrible urge to just sink down in a heap on the grass and cry.

But he couldn't. There were still people inside. Lauren was missing. Ignoring his aching muscles and raw lungs, he ran to the front of the house.

"Lauren!" he screamed. "Lauren!" His cries split the flaming night.

# ◼ HarperPaperbacks *By Mail*

Join KC, Faith, and Winnie as the three hometown friends share the triumphs, loves, and tragedies of their first year of college in this bestselling series:

# FRESHMAN DORM

## Away from home . . . and on their own!

**KC Angeletti:** Beautiful and talented, KC is a young woman on the move—and she'll do anything she can to succeed . . .

**Winnie Gottlieb:** Impulsive, reckless Winnie just can't keep her head on straight—how will she get through her first year?

**Faith Crowley:** Innocent Faith is Winnie and KC's best friend—but will she ever let loose and be her *own* friend?

**Follow all the joys and heartaches of the girls of Freshman Dorm!**

MAIL TO: Harper Collins Publishers
P.O. Box 588, Dunmore, PA 18512-0588
TELEPHONE: 1-800-331-3716
(Visa and Mastercard holders!)
YES, please send me the following titles:

❑ #1 Freshman Dorm (0-06-106000-3) ............... $3.50
❑ #2 Freshman Lies (0-06-106005-4) ................. $3.50
❑ #3 Freshman Guys (0-06-106011-9) ................. $3.50
❑ #4 Freshman Nights (0-06-106012-7) ............. $3.50
❑ #5 Freshman Dreams (0-06-106040-2) ............. $3.50
❑ #6 Freshman Games (0-06-106035-6) ............. $3.50
❑ #7 Freshman Loves (0-06-106048-8) ............. $3.50
❑ #8 Freshman Secrets (0-06-106034-8) ............. $3.50
❑ #9 Freshman Schemes (0-06-106086-0) ........... $3.50
❑ #10 Freshman Changes (0-06-106078-X) ......... $3.50
❑ #11 Freshman Fling (0-06-106121-2) ............. $3.50
❑ #12 Freshman Rivals (0-06-106122-0) ............. $3.50
❑ #13 Freshman Flames (0-06-106127-1) ............. $3.50
❑ #14 Freshman Choices (0-06-106128-X) ............. $3.50
❑ #15 Freshman Heartbreak (0-06-106140-9) ...... $3.50
❑ #16 Freshman Feud (0-06-106141-7) ............. $3.50

SUBTOTAL ............................................ $_____
POSTAGE AND HANDLING* ............... $ __2.00__
SALES TAX (Add applicable state sales tax) .... $_____

TOTAL: $_____
(Remit in U.S. funds. Do not send cash.)

NAME _____
ADDRESS _____
CITY _____
STATE _____ ZIP _____

Allow up to six weeks for delivery. Prices subject to change.
Valid only in U.S. and Canada.

◼ ***Free postage/handling if you buy four or more!***

H0331

# ♣ HarperPaperbacks *By Mail*

**Read all of the**
*Changes* R O M A N C E S
Discover yourself in the dramatic stories of the Changes
heroines as they face the same hopes and fears as you.

---

And look for these
other great series from
*HarperPaperbacks*:

## Mollie Fox Mysteries
**Created by Peter Nelson**
You've never seen danger
like this before . . .
And neither has Mollie
Fox, a hip, puzzle-solving
heroine for the nineties.
In this spellbinding new
series, join Mollie and her
friends as they unravel
one terrifying mystery
after another.

## The Vampire Diaries:
**A Trilogy by L.J. Smith**
Follow the terrifying story
of two vampire brothers
trapped in a dark love
triangle with a beautiful
mortal girl—and discover
the horrifying conclusion
in The Vampire Diaries
Volume IV Dark Reunion.

## Freshman Dorm
**By Linda A. Cooney**
Meet Faith, KC, and
Winnie as the three
hometown friends
experience the joys and
heartaches of their first
year of college. Now
seventeen titles strong!

MAIL TO: Harper Collins Publishers
P.O.Box 588, Dunmore, PA 18512-0588
TELEPHONE: 1-800-331-3716
(Visa and Mastercard holders!)
YES, please send me the following titles:

**Changes Romances**
❏ #1 My Phantom Love (0-06-106770-9) ............$3.50
❏ #2 Looking Out for Lacey (0-06-106772-5) ......$3.50
❏ #3 The Unbelievable Truth (0-06-106774-1) .....$3.50
❏ #4 Runaway (0-06-106782-2) ..........................$3.50
❏ #5 Cinderella Summer (0-06-106776-8) ...........$3.50

**Mollie Fox Mysteries**
❏ #1 First to Die (0-06-106100-X) .....................$3.50
❏ #2 Double Dose (0-06-106101-8)....................$3.50

**The Vampire Diaries**
❏ Vol. I  The Awakening (0-06-106097-6)............$3.99
❏ Vol. II The Struggle (0-06-106098-4)...............$3.99
❏ Vol. III The Fury (0-06-106099-2)...................$3.99
❏ Vol. IV Dark Reunion (0-06-106775-X) ............$3.99

**Freshman Dorm**
❏ #1 Freshman Dorm (0-06-106000-3) ...............$3.50
❏ #15 Freshman Heartbreak (0-06-106140-9)......$3.50
❏ #16 Freshman Feud (0-06-106141-7) ..............$3.50
❏ #17 Freshman Follies (0-06-106142-5) ............$3.50

SUBTOTAL ...........................................$_____
POSTAGE AND HANDLING* ................$  2.00
SALES TAX (Add applicable state sales tax) ....$_____

                                                    TOTAL:  $_____
                          (Remit in U.S. funds. Do not send cash.)

NAME_____
ADDRESS_____
CITY_____
STATE_____ ZIP _____
Allow up to six weeks for delivery. Prices subject to change.
Valid only in U.S. and Canada.

**\*Free postage/handling if you buy four or more!**

H0341